For Better or For Worse

"But how are you going to plan a whole wedding in a month?" Laurel asked.

"Yeah," I said. "The women on all those reality shows about weddings take like a year to plan theirs."

"Not to mention they have a lot of meltdowns and scream at people," Laurel added.

Mom shrugged. "There's really nothing to plan. It's just going to be the six of us—well, seven, including Ziggy. Very low-key. I mean, it's not like I'm really the wedding type." That was true. Mom was so laid-back that sometimes as a joke, Alan would grab her wrist and hold it and say he was feeling for a pulse. "Other than the fact that after I'm going to have to start checking the 'married' box again on questionnaires, it's i... be like any other day."

I looked at Laurel and p... shoulder. "Except that'll be th... become official fristers."

She smiled as she put her arm around mine.

Which, as far as I was concerned, would be the most awesome day of my life.

Books by Robin Palmer:

Yours Truly, Lucy B. Parker: Girl vs. Superstar
Yours Truly, Lucy B. Parker: Sealed with a Kiss
Yours Truly, Lucy B. Parker: Vote for Me!
Yours Truly, Lucy B. Parker: Take My Advice!
Yours Truly, Lucy B. Parker: For Better or For Worse

For teens:

Cindy Ella
Geek Charming
Little Miss Red
Wicked Jealous

Yours Truly,

For Better or For Worse

R O B I N   P A L M E R

PUFFIN BOOKS
An Imprint of Penguin Group (USA) Inc.

PUFFIN BOOKS
Published by the Penguin Group
Penguin Young Readers Group, 345 Hudson Street,
New York, New York 10014, U.S.A.
Penguin Group (Canada), 90 Eglinton Avenue East, Suite 700, Toronto,
Ontario, Canada M4P 2Y3 (a division of Pearson Penguin Canada Inc.)
Penguin Books Ltd, 80 Strand, London WC2R 0RL, England
Penguin Ireland, 25 St Stephen's Green, Dublin 2, Ireland
(a division of Penguin Books Ltd)
Penguin Group (Australia), 250 Camberwell Road, Camberwell,
Victoria 3124, Australia (a division of Pearson Australia Group Pty Ltd)
Penguin Books India Pvt Ltd, 11 Community Centre,
Panchsheel Park, New Delhi - 110 017, India
Penguin Group (NZ), 67 Apollo Drive, Rosedale,
Auckland 0632, New Zealand (a division of Pearson New Zealand Ltd)
Penguin Books (South Africa) (Pty) Ltd, 24 Sturdee Avenue,
Rosebank, Johannesburg 2196, South Africa

Penguin Books Ltd, Registered Offices: 80 Strand,
London WC2R 0RL, England

First published in the United States of America by Puffin Books and
G. P. Putnam's Sons, divisions of Penguin Young Readers Group, 2012

1 3 5 7 9 10 8 6 4 2

LIBRARY OF CONGRESS CATALOGING-IN-PUBLICATION DATA IS AVAILABLE

Puffin Books ISBN 978-0-14-241504-7

Printed in the United States of America

For Katie Malachuk,
a grown-up Lucy in all the best ways

Yours Truly,

Lucy B. PARKER

For Better or For Worse

chapter 1

Dear Dr. Maude,

I know that the last few (okay, more like twenty) e-mails I've written you, I've sometimes (okay, a lot of times) ended up mentioning the fact that you never write me back. Well, the reason I'm writing to you today is to tell you that when I say that, it's only because my teacher Mr. Eglington is always on us to "state the facts in a clear and concise manner" and that just happens to be a fact. But, the other day when I was watching this show on Animal Planet about female animals that completely IGNORE their babies—not even FEEDING them, which means that some surrogate animal has to do it or else they DIE OF STARVATION—for some weird reason it reminded me of you.

I started to worry that maybe the reason you haven't written me back is because you think when I say stuff like that—you know, the fact that I've been writing to you for more than a year and haven't gotten a SINGLE response—it's because I'm trying to make you feel guilty. But that is so not true. Like I said, I'm just stating the facts in a clear and concise manner. And, well, unfortunately, that's a fact.

Like I've ALSO said a bunch of times before, I wasn't

going to write to you anymore—especially not to ask you for advice—but now that I've gotten this far, I should probably just go ahead and do it this one last time. So my problem is this: Mom and Alan have been acting VERY weird the last few weeks. We're talking lots-of-conversations-behind-closed-doors-in-such-soft-voices-that-even-expert-overlisteners-like-myself-can't-overlisten. (As I've told you before, overlistening is not the same as eavesdropping. It's different.) And lots of closing their laptops very quickly whenever Laurel and I happen to walk by them. And lots of Mom, who's usually in a very good mood because she's a Buddhist, acting a little cranky. She even ended up gong to her shrink twice in one week instead of her usual one time.

Laurel and I have tried to figure it out, but so far we haven't been able to come up with anything other than maybe they're breaking up. There's no real reason why we think that would happen, except the fact that Laurel did a movie once where she played the daughter of a couple who was about to get divorced and they acted like this right before they told her.

I guess because we're a family that's so big on communicating, we could just call an emergency Parker-Moses Family Meeting and ask them what the heck is going on, but I'm afraid to do that. Because what if they ARE breaking up? Laurel and I have already decided that if that's the case, we're going to continue to be best friends and fristers anyway.

Obviously, this is a very important matter, so even though you've ignored all my other e-mails, if you could answer this one, I would appreciate it. Seeing that it's a life-and-death thing. Well, not a death thing exactly, but you know what I mean.

Thanks very much.

yours truly,
LUCY B. PARKER

"Maybe your mom is pregnant and that's why she's so cranky. According to one of my moms, pregnancy is like PMS times a hundred," my non-frister BFF Beatrice said as we ate lunch in Arizona the next day. Well, the area of the cafeteria that, if it were a map of the United States, would be Arizona. Becoming class president hadn't made me so popular that I had moved to Kansas (the state that was smack in the middle of the country and where the super-popular kids, like Cristina Pollock, sat), but at least I wasn't in Alaska anymore. Although the looks on our Colorado and Utah neighbors' faces once they got a whiff of Beatrice's sardine sandwich made it seem like they wished we were.

I shook my head as I swallowed a bite of my peanut butter and honey sandwich. It may have made my mouth stick together, but at least it didn't reek. "No. She's too old," I sighed. "Plus, whenever I ask that, she pats her stomach and says, 'This store is closed.'"

After Sarah got pregnant with Ziggy, my biggest fear was that Mom was going to go ahead and have a baby, too. That was back when I didn't really like babies because I had never held one before and I was afraid I'd drop them. But once Ziggy was born, I discovered I had this crazy baby-whispering talent where I could make them stop crying the minute I picked them up. Because I wasn't good at singing or anything coordination-oriented, I considered the baby-whispering thing my second official talent after advice giving (I had a column in the school paper). Which is why I decided I wouldn't have been all that upset if Mom did get pregnant.

"Oh! Oh! I know!" gasped Alice, my next non-frister BFF after Beatrice. As she bounced up and down in her chair, a meatball fell out of her sub and rolled off the table, just missing my next, next non-frister BFF Malia's leg. Because Alice was what Alan called "an overexcitable type," she could be very dangerous to eat with. "Whoops. Sorry," she said to Malia. "Wait a second—what was I just saying?" she asked after she picked up the meatball.

"You were saying 'Oh! Oh! I know!'" Malia replied in a very Alice-sounding voice. Although she was much more into drawing (with two parents who were artists, she had been lucky enough to inherit that talent from them), I was always telling her that she should try out for the school play because she was great at acting.

"Oh right," Alice said. After pushing her tray into the middle of the table, she began to bounce up and down again. "Oh! Oh! I know!" she gasped as Beatrice rolled her eyes and shook her head. As a born and bred New Yorker, Beatrice had no problem saying what was on her mind at all times—even if it was just with her expressions. When we were first becoming friends it was a little intimidating, but after we had known each other a while, I realized that someone saying "You have a booger hanging from your nose" was a lot more helpful than someone who was so afraid of hurting your feelings that she let you walk into the cafeteria like that.

"What?" I asked.

"What what?" Alice replied, confused.

This time I was the one who rolled my eyes. Partly because, after eight months of living in Manhattan, I was on my way to becoming a New Yorker. And partly because you had to be like a nun or a super-duper mellow yoga person to *not* get annoyed with Alice. "We were talking about my mom, and why she might be cranky, and you said 'Oh! Oh! I know!' in a way that made it seem like you knew."

"Oh right. Now I remember," she said. "What I was going to say was maybe your mom is really a *spy*. From, like, *Russia* or something. And she didn't mean to fall in love with Alan but she did. And once the president of Russia found out he got *really* mad and now she's not allowed to go back there or else they'll *kill* her.

This time even Malia—who was pretty much the nicest person I had ever met— rolled her eyes.

"Okay, (a) my mother isn't a Russian spy—"

"How do you know?" Alice interrupted. "She could be. Just because she speaks perfect English and doesn't have an accent doesn't mean anything. Spies are expert actors. In fact, maybe that's why she started going out with Alan—so she could learn acting tips from Laurel."

I shook my head. "You know what? That's just so crazy I'm not even going to go to (b)," I said.

Beatrice patted my hand. "Don't worry, Lucy—if they do split up and you have to move back to Northampton, we'll come visit you."

"Sure," Alice said. "We won't forget about you like that girl what's-her-name who moved away before fifth grade." She turned to Beatrice. "What was her name again? The really nice one who wore headgear at night?"

Beatrice shrugged. "I don't remember."

I hadn't even thought about that part. If Mom and Alan split up, would we move back to Northampton? Granted Dad and Ziggy and Sarah were there, but I felt like New York was my home now. Plus, I had only recently stopped being the New Girl. I wasn't ready to become a What's-Her-Name again.

"Okay, this is not good," I said.

"I have an idea," Malia said. "If you were giving yourself advice about this situation, what would you tell yourself?"

I thought about it. Advice was definitely something I knew about. After the original advice columnist for our school newspaper got fired for plagiarism, I ended up taking over the job, and it turned out I had a real knack for it. So much so that when the trial period was over, Dr. Remington-Wallace, our principal, extended my contract. Although I had been using the pseudonym of "Annie" at first, I decided to come out and let everyone know it was me, mostly because as class president I felt that keeping my identity secret, while not exactly a lie, wasn't the best example to put out there.

"I would tell myself...that this is not good," I replied.

"But you can't move!" Laurel cried that night from her bed before dinner after I told her about the conversation at lunch.

"It's not like I want to!" I cried back as I paced around her very neat, not-a-thing-out-of-place bedroom. I tried to ignore the fact that my ten-year-old cat, Miss Piggy, was curled up in Laurel's lap, purring so loud they probably heard it all the way across the Atlantic Ocean in France. Or at least a few floors down in Beatrice's apartment.

Even though I was the one who fed Miss Piggy and scooped her litter box and cleaned up her yakked-up hairballs and gave her Greenie treats, she had never really liked me. And when Laurel had come into the picture? Forget it. Suddenly, she started sleeping in Laurel's room (I had to lock my door to get Miss Piggy to stay in mine) and cuddling with her. (When I tried to force her to cuddle, all I got were hisses and scratches.)

That was why a few months earlier I had launched Operation New Kitten in order to get a pet that I could train to actually like me. As if to try and make me feel worse, Miss Piggy burrowed down deeper into Laurel's lap and began to make biscuits on her legs. Although Mom said that cats didn't know how to give dirty looks, Miss Piggy sure did. And she also knew how to smile. Well, at Laurel.

I stopped pacing. "Wow. You really do look blind," I said, impressed.

Laurel focused her eyes. "I do?! Thanks," she said with a smile before she unfocused them again.

Ever since Laurel had signed on to do this new movie called *Life Is What Happens When You're Making Other Plans* she had been obsessed with getting into character, which explained why she looked blind. According to her agent, Marv, and her publicist, Marci, Laurel was going to win an Academy Award for the movie. Even though it hadn't even started shooting (not until next spring) they were all very sure about this fact.

When I first started living with Laurel, I had loved reading her scripts. Not only were they interesting, but I was super flattered that she cared about my opinion. But because she was offered like five movies a week, and the scripts were over a hundred pages, that was a lot of reading—even for someone like me who enjoyed reading. So now I only read the ones that she was seriously considering.

I loved *Life* (it got tiring saying *Life Is What Happens When You're Making Other Plans*) right away. First of all, it was based on a quote by John Lennon, my favorite Beatle. (The exact quote was "Life is what happens to you while you're busy making other plans," which is even more exhausting to say.) But even if had had a different title, I still would've liked it. By the time I was done reading it, I had laughed and cried so many different times I felt like I needed a nap.

The movie was about was this girl named Jenny who goes blind and, instead of being sad about it, decides to make a list of one hundred things she wants to do before she dies and then sets out to do them all. In the end, she gets an eye transplant and can see again, so while it's sad for a lot of the movie, it ends up being happy on account of the fact that people in Hollywood are really big on happy endings. Although I didn't like Laurel's publicist, Marci, because she had gotten mad at me on the set of Laurel's movie in L.A. after I had mistakenly talked to a reporter who I didn't know was a reporter, I had to agree with her when she said that it was one of the best scripts she'd ever read.

"But the Oscars won't be half as great if you're not sitting next to me," Laurel said. "Plus, if you move, you'll have to find a whole new official local crush."

Oh no. I hadn't even thought about that. I sighed. This whole Three-Crush Rule was a major pain in the butt. When Beatrice and I became friends, she had informed me that it was common knowledge that everyone had to have three: a local one; a long distance/vacation one; and a celebrity one. Although we didn't have this back in Northampton, apparently this was a well-known fact in New York. So well known that, according to Malia, they even knew about it in Italy, which is where she lived before moving to New York and replacing me as the New Girl. That's why I had decided it was log-worthy and had become the Keeper of the Crushes with my official log called "The Official Crush Log of the Girls at the Center for Creative Learning in New York, NY." (I had another log as well—"The Official Period Log of the Girls at the Center for Creative Learning in New York, NY," which, sadly, my name had yet to be entered in.)

Frankly, I didn't know what the big deal about boys was. It wasn't like you could go do fun stuff with crushes like you did with your friends such as play TWUO (The World's Ugliest Outfit). Plus, even the really cute ones who showered on a daily basis gave off this funky boy smell that was a mix of chicken noodle soup and wet socks.

That being said, because of all the pressure being put on me to come up with my picks, I had recently decided on Beatrice's brother, Blair, as my local crush. Although he played chess, talked with his mouth full, and had food stains on his clothes, the fact that he lived only a few floors below me in our apartment building made him extremely local. I had even gone as far as to ask him to the Sadie

Hawkins dance that my school recently had (the girls had to ask the boys, which was awful). He couldn't go, but he had said in an e-mail to me that we'd go do something some other time. Which I was still waiting for.

Before Laurel and I could figure out what to do to stop Mom and Alan from breaking up, there was a knock on the door.

"Come in," Laurel called out. "Wait…I mean…come in," she said in a depressed, just-found-out-she's-blind voice. She turned to me. "How was that?"

As I gave her a thumbs-up, Alan poked his head in. "Sorry for the short notice, but I wanted to let you girls know there will be an emergency Parker-Moses Family Meeting at seven p.m. tonight. I'll send out an Outlook invite as well so it's synced on your computer devices."

Laurel and I looked at each, panicked. The breakup was happening even faster than we had thought.

"And Brian and Sarah will be joining us via Skype, so we'll be starting right on the dot."

We looked at each other again, even more freaked out. My dad and his girlfriend, Sarah, were included in this? Probably to talk about me moving back to Northampton.

This was not good.

"You did *what*?!" Laurel gasped after Alan and Mom told us the big news.

11

"We set a date for the wedding," Alan replied. "A month from Saturday at the Black Horse Inn in Cabot Village, Vermont."

"Population two hundred thirty-nine," Mom added excitedly. "And home of the world-famous Cabot Creamery."

"Supposedly their cheddar cheese is out of this world," Alan said.

"It's about six hours from here," Mom added.

"Six hours and ten minutes," Alan corrected. "Or 329.38 miles, however you want to look at it."

"Wait a minute—so you're not breaking up?" I asked.

"What?" Mom asked, confused.

"Nothing. Forget it," I said.

"Oh, that's terrific!" Dad cried from through the computer. "We're so happy for you."

Thinking I heard a sniffle, I squinted and leaned into the computer. "Dad, are you crying?" I asked.

He wiped his eyes. "Yes. They're tears of joy, Lucy."

While I knew I was lucky to have parents who very rarely yelled at me, the fact that my dad wasn't the least bit embarrassed to cry in front of people was a little bit weird.

"And, Brian, we have a favor we'd like to ask you," Mom said.

"We were wondering if you'd officiate at the ceremony," Alan continued.

"Really?" Dad asked. About a year before he had become an ordained minister through the Internet so he could perform the wedding for Sarah's friends Seth and Marc. It seemed a little strange that for $39.95 anyone could do it, but seeing that it came with a certificate and everything, I guess it was official.

As Mom and Alan nodded, more tears came. "I'd be honored," Dad said.

Obviously, I was glad that Mom and Alan weren't breaking up for a bunch of reasons—one of them being that I still hadn't fully recovered from the packing and unpacking that came with the move from Northampton to Manhattan. But I had to say the fact that my mother was asking my father to handle the wedding ceremony to her new husband was just plain *weird*. Although, given my family, "weird" was the new normal.

As I watched Mom beam at Alan, though, I forgave her for any weirdness. The truth was that as organized and nervous as Alan could be, I had never seen her so happy. They loved each other a lot, but not in the totally crazy way that the people on the telenovela that I liked to watch with our housekeeper, Rose, after school. (Rose was from Jamaica, and she didn't speak Spanish, either. But once you watched the shows for a while, it was easy enough to catch on. Basically, they all had the same things as American soap operas: people falling in love with people who were already married to someone else and people coming back from the dead.) As Mom once put it, she and Alan were "best friends who enjoyed kissing each other."

This is going to be fantastic!" Sarah said. "Hey, I know a shaman up in that area. Maybe he could come and do some sort of blessing." In addition to being a yoga teacher, Sarah was into all sorts of crazy stuff like blessing and using sticky essential oils to cure everything from backaches to period cramps. (When mine finally came, I guess I'd give that a try.) "He's great with that kind of thing. Except you have to supply your own birds' beaks and stuff like that. Or maybe my mom could come from Arizona!"

Uh-oh. I had met Sarah's mom at Ziggy's baby shower and she was bonkers. We're talking the-woman-thought-her-house-had-been-hit-with-a-spaceship kind of bonkers.

Mom and Alan looked at each other nervously. "Uh, that's interesting, Sarah," Mom said. "Why don't we talk about that some other time?"

Like, say, never.

"I can't believe you finally agreed on a place," Laurel said.

"Neither can we," Mom replied.

While Mom and Alan had a lot in common—such as the fact that they both loved movies directed by some guy named Woody Allen—they were also very different in a lot of ways. Like the fact that Mom enjoyed hikes and nature while Alan got totally freaked out if there was a fly in the apartment. It was bad enough when they had been trying to pick a place to go for their one-year anniversary (and even worse when I got involved and almost totally screwed it up), but the whole where-to-get-married thing had been a nightmare.

"I think the Black Horse Inn will be perfect," Alan said. "It's very pretty and has a country feel, but according to the brochures, you can still get cell phone reception and the *New York Times*. Plus, I checked the Old Farmer's Almanac, and even though we'll be into November, there's no snow in the forecast for that weekend."

"But how are you going to plan a whole wedding in a month?" Laurel asked.

"Yeah," I said. "The women on all those reality shows about weddings take like a year to plan theirs."

"Not to mention they have a lot of meltdowns and scream at people," Laurel added.

Mom shrugged. "There's really nothing to plan. It's just going to be the six of us—well, seven, including Ziggy. Very low-key. I mean, it's not like I'm really the wedding type." That was true. Mom was so laid-back that sometimes as a joke, Alan would grab her wrist and hold it and say he was feeling for a pulse. "Other than the fact that after I'm going to have to start checking the 'married' box again on questionnaires, it's just going to be like any other day."

I looked at Laurel and put my arm around her shoulder. "Except that'll be the day that Laurel and I become official fristers."

She smiled as she put her arm around mine.

Which, as far as I was concerned, would be the most awesome day of my life.

Well, at least until I finally got my period.

"There's something we wanted to ask you girls, though—" Alan said.

"—we wanted to know if you would give the toast at the reception," Mom finished.

Mom and Alan did that a lot—finished each other's sentences. I wondered if that was something that all couples did and if I ever had a boyfriend, if I'd end up doing that, too. (I actually hoped I wouldn't. Because if I could finish his sentences, that would mean I'd know what he was thinking, which, frankly, would be pretty boring. Except around the holidays or my birthday when I could psychically tell what he was getting me for a gift.) Sarah did that to Dad a lot, too. But she also did that me, so in that case it was just an annoying interrupting habit thing versus a couple thing.

Laurel and I looked at each other and smiled. That would be awesome. Ever since becoming class president I had gotten a lot more comfortable with public speaking. Like to the point where I no longer had to use the tricks Laurel had taught me about imagining people in their underwear in order to take away my nerves.

Although I had to admit I was a little worried that if Laurel and I were going to give a toast together, she might end up hogging the whole thing. For the most part she was super generous (when she shared the swag from the kind of goodie bags she got from the parties she went to, it was along the lines of designer jeans and

16

Ugg boots rather than glitter pens and SweeTarts). But sometimes when it came to stuff in front of an audience, she couldn't stop the performer in her from coming out. Like when we ended up at a karaoke place during our first group date with Mom and Alan and she went to town signing "Beautiful" by Christina Aguilera complete with hair flips as if she was a special guest judge on *The Voice* or something. (As for me, I sang The Beatles' "Let It Be," complete with microphone feedback and my mother having to help me out because I'm pretty much tone-deaf.)

"That's so nice of you to ask us," Laurel said. "But I think Lucy should do it herself."

I looked at her. "You do?"

She nodded. "Yeah. You're really the writer in the family."

I smiled. With all the hundreds of scripts she had read over the years, that was a big compliment coming from her. And with all the experience I was getting with my advice column, I was getting pretty good at coming up with clever things to say without her help.

"Of course, I can look it over for spelling and grammatical errors," she added.

Of course she could. And of course she would. Laurel may have been on the Best Dressed Teen lists of every magazine and dating Austin Mackenzie, her male equivalent in the teen heartthrob department, but what most people didn't know was that if there was an

Academy Award for Most Organized and a Total Stickler for Things Being Just So, Laurel would've won it hands down. I, on the other hand, was a little (okay, a lot) on the less-organized side—and that included not running spell-check when I wrote something.

"That would be great," I replied with a smile.

When Laurel and I had first met, I was afraid that the fact that we were so different was going to be a huge problem, but it actually had turned out to be a really good thing.

If anyone had told me a year earlier that I would be living in New York City, with the most famous girl in the world, about to write a toast to read on the day that she and I officially became fristers, I never would've believed it.

But I was. And I had to say, other than the fact that my boobs wouldn't stop growing and my period still hadn't gotten here, my life was pretty awesome.

chapter 2

Dear Dr. Maude,

Okay, you are SO not going to believe the huge news that I have!!!

It turns out that Mom and Alan aren't splitting up. Instead they're finally getting married! Which means that in one month Laurel and I will OFFICIALLY be fristers. I'm excited about it for a bunch of reasons (getting to buy a new dress ... wedding cake ... getting to give the toast ... no longer having to explain, "Well, we're not officially fristers yet, but we will be once our parents get their act together and set a date" ... wedding cake).

Last night before I went to bed, after getting yelled at by Mom for typing this on my iTouch when I was supposed to be sleeping, I thought about how freaked out I had been when Mom first told me she was dating Alan. You remember how worried I had been that Laurel was going to end up getting all the attention because she's so famous and talented while I'm so normal and uncoordinated, right? Actually, you'd only know that if you had read my e-mails.

Anyway, that hasn't happened. If anything, living with Laurel has been great because it's showed me that just because someone's life might look really awesome on the outside, you never know how they feel on the inside. Like the fact that Laurel gets very easily freaked out about things such as germs and messiness and tends to worry a lot.

And Alan is an awesome frather. (That's friend + father instead of stepfather.) I mean, to organize a whole dance for me at home because he felt bad for me that my official local crush, Blair Lerner-Moskovitz, couldn't go to the Sadie Hawkins one with me? That is soooo sweet. Even if his taste in music is kind of dorky (he played a song by these two old people Neil Diamond and Barbra Streisand) and we ended up just going for ice cream instead.

Plus, guess what? Dad and Sarah and Ziggy get to come, too, because Dad's performing the ceremony. I haven't seen a lot of ministers in my life because my parents are Buddhists and are letting me choose my own religion, but I have seen a bunch of them on TV as I've flipped the channels to get to Animal Planet, and none of them had ponytails like Dad does. In fact, the ones who are Buddhist monks have shaved heads.

Okay, well, I'm going to go look at dresses on the Urban Outfitters website to wear to the wedding now.

yours truly,
LUCY B. PARKER

In movies and TV shows, after someone announces they're getting married, it seems like people go nuts and the speed revs up and everything gets super fast. Kind of like if you push the "4x" fast-forward button on the DVD remote control. Suddenly, all people can talk about is the wedding, which means all the other important things in life (i.e., the fact that you feel that your parents should really, really, REALLY let you get a kitten due to the fact that your cat that you take very good care of hates you) are put on hold.

But in the Parker-Moses family, the wedding was barely discussed. Well, at least by my mom. Which meant that she had all the time in the world to tell me yet again that no matter how many times I asked about the kitten, the answer was still no and that because Miss Piggy was family, she and I were going to have to use our conflict-resolution skills to work out whatever issues we were having. Which, if Miss Piggy had spoken English instead of Catese, may have worked, but she didn't.

"Look at it this way," I said to Mom as she and I made our way through Central Park during our IBS (IBS = Individual Bonding Session = something Alan had come up with when we blended our families) a few afternoons later after she picked me up at the Center for Creative Learning, my school on the Upper East Side. "Weddings are all about new beginnings and commitment. And what better way to celebrate a new beginning than committing to a cute baby kitten!"

Laurel had helped me come up with that the night before. When she suggested it, I was afraid that it sounded a little TV commercial-like (which is why I agreed that it was good that I was taking care of the speech). But it was better than what I was planning on saying, which was "The reason I want a kitten is because it really hurts my feelings to watch Miss Piggy act like some starstruck fan whenever she's around Laurel." Even though that was true.

Mom shook her head. "Nice try, but no."

I sighed. "Fine. If you're not going to let me get a kitten, will you at least let me go wedding dress shopping with you?" Unlike most women, Mom hated to shop. But the good news is that when she did go, and I went with her, she always let me get something, too. And there was a pair of polka-dot Converse hi-tops that had just come out that I really, really, *really* wanted and didn't feel like waiting until Kwaanza for. (Because Mom was Buddhist, Alan was Jewish, and Laurel and I had been raised with no religion, in one of our family meetings about the holidays, we had taken a vote and decided we would celebrate a neutral holiday.)

She shook her head. "I'm not buying a wedding dress."

"What are you talking about? You have to!"

"How come?" she asked.

I thought about it. Why was she asking *me*? *I* had never been married. "Well, because, it's … the *weddingly* thing to do," I finally said.

She turned to me. "Says who? Fashion designers and magazines who want to force women to spend their hard-earned money on overpriced garments for which they end up almost starving themselves to get into so that they can fulfill some fantasy that was thrust upon them in childhood by the fairy tales that were read to them about waiting around for a prince to come save them?"

Uh-oh. Mom had just stepped up on what Alan called her soapbox, which, because I had never seen one, I figured was something they used to have in the old days. While she may have been laid back, Mom was what my dad's mom called a "feminist" (although the way she said it made it sound like it wasn't a great thing to be). When it came to women's rights, Mom tended to go on and on and her face got red as she talked.

"Mom, I'm twelve," I replied. "And that's a lot of syllables for me to take in when I haven't had my after-school snack yet."

She laughed and ruffled my brown hair. Which, thankfully, was on its way to medium-long-dom versus super-short-dom—something I feared would never happen after the Straightening Iron Incident before the start of sixth grade. I overshot the mark by holding the straightening iron on my pigtail too long in an attempt to get rid of my curls. "You're right," Mom said. "It's just that I don't want to make a big deal about this day. It's like Valentine's Day," she explained. "I just never understood why you're supposed to love someone more on that day versus the other 364. And a wedding is the same kind of thing."

I guess she had a point, but hopefully she wouldn't mind if I dressed up because I had found three really awesome dresses on the Urban Outfitters website the other night.

"As far as I'm concerned, everything's just business as usual," she said.

Well, it was business as usual until Marissa got involved by being all Marissaish and stirring things up. Marissa was a friend of mine from Northampton. I wasn't sure who was more annoying: her or Alice.

It started the next afternoon, as we were having our weekly Triple S. Triple S stood for Skype Snack Session and was something that I had originally started with the actor Connor Forrester, whom I had met out in L.A. when I was there with Laurel. Much to everyone's surprise (no one more than mine) I ended up having my first kiss with Connor. It wasn't like we became all boyfriend/ girlfriend after that, though. Super-cute teen superstar + me = weird combination. He was nice but a little too goofy for me, which was why we were just friends. That totally bummed Laurel out because Connor also happened to be her boyfriend Austin's BFF. ("Two BFFs dating two BFFs?! How cute would that be?!" she cried.)

I didn't even like Connor enough in that way to have him as my celebrity crush, let alone my long-distance/vacation one. Even though, given all the trouble I was having coming up with crush ideas, being able to use him in both categories would have been very helpful for the log.

When Marissa heard about the Triple S's she did this whole "Ooh! Ooh! I loooooove that soooooo much!" thing before texting me five times a day saying, "I want to have a Triple S, too! Can we? Please? Please? Let me know IMMEDIATELY." I ignored her for two days until I couldn't take it anymore and finally caved and said yes.

With Connor the Triple S's were fun (except when he played his guitar, which he liked to think he was really good at, but actually was not), as were the ones with Ziggy. You'd think that Skyping with a baby would be boring on account of the fact that they pretty much just lie there and try and eat their toes. Even though he couldn't talk yet, I was pretty sure that from the little noises he made throughout our conversation Ziggy totally understood what I was saying.

But the Triple S's with Marissa were beyond painful. Part of it was because she was a very loud eater, which meant that I could hear every crunch of every SunChip, her favorite snack (at least I couldn't smell it, which was good seeing that she liked the French Onion flavor the best). And part of it was because every few minutes she would lean into the computer camera and yell, "YOU

CAN REALLY SEE ME THROUGH THIS?" and I'd say, "Yes, Marissa, I can see you." And then she'd yell, "AND YOU CAN HEAR ME, TOO? ARE YOU SURE? BECAUSE IF YOU WANT I CAN SPEAK LOUDER?" And I'd say, "That's okay, Marissa. You don't need to speak louder. In fact, you might want to speak a little softer so that I'm only a little deaf rather than completely." And then she'd say, "WHAT DID YOU SAY? I CAN'T HEAR YOU. OMIGOD—DO YOU THINK I'M LOSING MY HEARING?" until I wrote on a piece of notebook paper *Try unmuting the Mute button* and held it up to the camera. And then sometimes, depending on what kind of mood I was in, I ended up "accidentally" disconnecting the Skype thing for a few minutes because a person can only deal with someone so annoying for so long.

"OMIGOD, I STILL CAN'T BELIEVE THEY FINALLY SET A DATE!" Marissa shrieked into the computer as she crunched on SunChips.

"Yup. They did," I replied for like the tenth time as I turned the volume down so it was almost off.

"THAT IS SOOOOO COOL!" she shrieked again. She was so loud that Miss Piggy looked up from the floor where she was grooming herself and glared at the computer before hissing at me.

I looked at her. "What did *I* do?"

"You know, Lucy, I hate to point this out because it will probably hurt your feelings, but Miss Piggy never really liked you," Marissa said. "Even before you moved

26

in with Laurel and she started sleeping on Laurel's bed because she wanted to, not because she was being forced to because the door was locked and she couldn't get out—"

"Can we talk about something else?" I said.

"Sure. Let me think. Ummmmmmmmmmmm . . ."

I cringed. Marissa could draw an *umm* out for MINUTES.

She began to jump up and down in her chair. "Oh! Oh! I know!" she cried. "We can talk about me coming to the wedding!"

I shook my head. "Sorry," I said. "It's family only."

"But I'm *kind* of family," she said. "You know, because I'm Ziggy's babysitter." I don't know what my father had been thinking when he finally agreed to let Marissa watch Ziggy. He said that she was very good at the job because she really paid attention to Ziggy, unlike other babysitters who just zoned out in front of the TV and let the baby cry until a commercial. But, still, exposing Ziggy to that much annoying behavior at such an early age could cause permanent damage. "That makes us almost related," she added.

Yeah, about as related as I was to Mr. Kim, the Korean guy who owned the deli down the street. "Nope. Mom's being really strict about all this," I replied. She really was. It was kind of weird.

"And there's also the fact that I used to be your best friend before you moved away and Cass became my best friend," she added. "By the way, I know we've never talked about this, but I hope me being best friends with her didn't hurt your feelings too much. At one point Cass and I talked about maybe you joining us in BFFdom, but Cass didn't think it was a good match. "

Okay, (a) Marissa and I were *never* best friends, even after my BFFs Rachel and Missy dumped me right before sixth grade started and she and I were the only ones in our class who didn't have one and she kept nagging me about it every day. And (b) I had met this Cass person when I was back in Northampton over the summer and she was right—we were definitely not a match. I didn't even want to be *friends*, let alone BFFs, with that girl.

Plus, the fact that she and Marissa had decided like five hours after meeting each other that they were BFFs ("It was like love at first sight—but with friendship!" Marissa had cried) seemed awfully fast to me. In fact, if Beatrice and I ever got around to writing the guide to BFFdom that we kept talking about, I was going to make sure to include something about how you had to be friends with someone for at least six weeks before having the BFF talk, which was the amount of time me and Beatrice had waited.

"So the ex-BFF thing also makes us kind of related," Marissa said.

"Yeah, kind of but not really," I replied. "Listen, Marissa, I hate to do this but I just remembered I have to go"— I looked around the room as I tried to come up with a good excuse until my eyes landed on Miss Piggy, who was still glaring at me. Although I was very careful not to actually discuss Operation New Kitten in front of her, it seemed to me that, recently, she had been giving me more dirty looks, which had led me to believe that she might be psychic —"feed Miss Piggy."

"But Miss Piggy doesn't get fed until eight," Marissa said. "Remember? Because if you do it earlier, then she gets really bad gas and ends up farting all through dinner and then everyone loses their appetites?"

At that, I could have sworn that Miss Piggy raised her eyebrow at the computer. At least I wasn't the only person she got annoyed with. I sighed. That's what I got for lying to someone who had taken care of my cat whenever we were on vacation. "Right. Well, then I have to—"

"So has The Change started?" Marissa asked as I wracked my brain for a non-lie excuse.

"The what?"

"You know—The *Change*. The thing that happens in blended families after the wedding," she replied. There's a lot that Marissa says that you can't believe because she has this way of always messing up the facts. (Marissa: "Did you know that an elephant is only pregnant for twenty-two *days* before she has the baby?!" Me: "Um, it's twenty-two *months*, Marissa. Which makes it the longest gestation period for any mammal. I saw that special on Animal Planet, too.") But because Marissa's parents had gotten divorced a few years before mine and then her mom married this guy named Phil who spent most of his time sitting in a recliner drinking beer and watching TV, she had more experience with the blended family stuff than I did.

Marissa had been the one who had explained to me that when a parent was dating someone and they said, "Things are getting serious," that meant it was only a matter of time before they became engaged to that person. Which was exactly what happened with Mom and Alan.

"But they haven't gotten married yet."

"Yeah, I know. But because Alan's so organized I thought it may have started early."

"Yeah, but what is it?" I asked as a family of Mexican jumping beans began to dance in my stomach. "You never mentioned this Change thing before."

"I didn't? Huh. That's weird. I'm surprised. You know, 'cause it's such a big deal and all."

The jumping beans turned into trapeze artists. I leaned in closer to the computer. "Marissa—what's The Change?!" I panicked.

Marissa moved back. "Gosh, Lucy. You don't have to *yell*."

"Okay, sorry. But you need to tell me what The Change is!"

"And by the way, because we were once best friends, I feel like I can tell you this," she went on. "You have something hanging from your nose. I don't think it's an actual booger, but it's booger-*like*."

I swiped at it. "Marissa, if you don't tell me what The Change is right this second I'm going to have to—"

"Tell people that I stuff my bra?" she asked anxiously. "You wouldn't do that, would you? Because that would be really mean. Plus, ever since I started using socks instead of toilet paper it looks a lot more real," she babbled. "And when I use knee socks instead of peds, my boobs are almost as big as yours!"

I rolled my eyes. "No, Marissa. I won't tell people you stuff your bra." When it came to boob stuff, I was very sensitive to other people's feelings on account of the fact that my mother was *not* and had no problem announcing in front of anyone how much mine had grown and how many times I had already outgrown my bras since getting my first one almost a year ago.

"Okay, good. Phew," she sighed. "So what was it we were talking about?"

"We were talking about this Change thing!"

"Oh right."

"So what is it?"

"What's what?"

After I was done banging my head on the desk, I looked at her. "The. *Change*."

Even Miss Piggy had stopped grooming herself and looked interested.

"Oh. The Change is when, after the wedding, everyone

31

stops being on their best behavior and goes back to being who they really are," she explained. "So parents stop treating all the kids equal and start choosing favorites. Like how, right after the wedding, both Phil and my mom started getting all 'Marissa, why can't you be more like your sister?'"

I didn't say it, because it would have been mean, but Marissa would probably have a lot more friends if she *had* been more like her sister, on account of the fact that her sister is only slightly, rather than completely, annoying. "Well, I don't think that's going to happen here," I said nervously. "I already had a conversation with my mom about that stuff back when we first moved here and she wasn't paying attention to me and it got all figured out."

Marissa shrugged. "Okay, but don't say I didn't warn you." She looked at her watch. "I have to go. *Week with Wendi* is about to start."

Week with Wendi was Marissa's favorite show. In it, Wendi Wallerstein followed different celebrities around for a week so that the audience got to see what they were like in their real life. It was kind of like the *Stars—They're Just Like Us!* part of *US Weekly* but in 3-D. Because everything that Wendi said sounded like it had an exclamation point after it, it made sense that Marissa liked it. I myself would have rather watched something on Animal Planet, or, even better, *Hoarders.*

"Okay. Bye," I said glumly. I looked over at Miss Piggy.

"Have *you* heard anything about this Change stuff?" I asked her.

All I got was a hiss in return.

I sighed. Now a new kitten—*that* would be one change I'd look forward to.

When I first found out that Dr. Maude and I were neighbors, I thought I was set for life. Not only would I be able to get free advice whenever I wanted, but I'd also get to walk her two dachshunds, Id and Ego, through Central Park because we lived right across the street from it. Unfortunately, I was wrong on both counts.

In the whole time I had lived there I hadn't run into her *once*—not even on the days when I found myself right in front of her door even though we lived on different floors. (Beatrice called it stalking, but I liked to think of it as exploring my surroundings in case I was elected fire drill captain for the building.)

Which meant that when it came to asking for advice from a non-family–related adult, I went to Pete, my doorman. From the minute he had offered me Gummy Worms—my favorite candy—when I moved in, Pete had pretty much been my BFF, adult-wise. And because he had been a doorman for so long, Pete knew a lot of stuff about a lot of stuff. ("I'm a doorman—we know these things" was something he said about ten times a day.) He was also big on giving the advice to "just be yourself," which, frankly, I wasn't completely sold on because of the fact that it just seemed so ... easy. Even though when I followed that advice—which usually didn't happen until after I screwed things up by *not* being myself—everything seemed to work out.

Because he had been a doorman for so long, Pete had seen more than his share of people getting divorced and then remarried, so I figured that if anyone had witnessed The Change firsthand, it was him.

"Pete, I need to ask you something," I said after I got down to the lobby and found him double-checking the FedEx and delivery log he kept of all the packages and dry cleaning that had arrived that day for the people in the building.

"And I need to ask *you* something," he said, opening his desk drawer and taking out a package of Gummi Worms. "Worm?" he asked, holding them out.

I took a few and settled in on the couch. "Thanks. Okay, you go first."

"So last night, on my way home, as I took the N train back into Astoria"—Astoria was in Queens, another borough of New York. I had taken the N there once, by mistake, when I had first moved here, and got totally lost. Thankfully, Laurel had come to rescue me because that's where the studio was where she shot her TV show *The World According to Madison Tennyson* "—I was thinking—"

Uh-oh. I settled back into the couch. When Pete started thinking, he could go on for a very long time.

"—about how I'm not very happy that Blair Lerner-Moskovitz *still* hasn't gotten it together and asked you to go do something after sending you that e-mail."

I cringed. Because of the adult BFF thing, Pete pretty much knew everything about my life. Maybe it was time to rethink that. Especially because even with all his doorman knowledge, one thing he *didn't* know was how to keep his voice down when talking about crushes. "Pete!" I cried.

"What? Am I talking too loud again about your crush on Blair Lerner-Moskovitz?" he asked in just as loud of a voice. So loud that snoopy old Mrs. McDonald from 8B turned around from the wall of mailboxes to see who the crusher was. According to Pete, Mrs. McDonald was very bad news. He couldn't prove it, but he was pretty sure that it was her who had tried to sell our garbage to one of the gossip magazines that had a "Stars—Their Garbage Is Just Like Ours!" section so she could make some money.

"(A) yes. Yes you are," I said. "And (b) it's B.L.M., remember?"

"Right. B.L.M. for Blair Lerner-Moskovitz," he said.

Yup. Definitely rethinking how much to share with Pete from now on. "And (c), no he has not. Not that I've thought about it all that much." Okay, fine, that was a bit of a lie. The truth was that sometimes, right before I fell asleep, I'd pop up in bed and think: *Wait a minute—after I asked Blair to the Sadie Hawkins dance and he couldn't go, he said we'd go do something. But he still hasn't asked me to do anything, even though I've now run into him five times at his apartment when I was hanging out with Beatrice.*

Pete shook his head. "I might have to talk to that boy," he said. "You don't just send a girl an e-mail asking her to do something and then not follow through."

"I know," I agreed. "If only because it'll give you bad karma."

"And if you're Blair Lerner-Moskovitz—sorry, I meant *B.L.M*—you *really* don't do it."

He was too nice to say anything mean, but I knew that Pete thought it was weird that of all the boys in the world, I had chosen Blair as my local crush. It wasn't like I *wanted* to have a crush on a former president of the AV Club/current member of the Upper West Side Chess Club. But out of all the boys I knew, he was the most decent choice I could come up with.

"Can I talk about my thing now?" I asked, changing the subject.

"Sure."

"Okay. So do you know anything about this thing called The Change?"

"You mean The Change that happens in blended families after the wedding happens and it's all official?" he asked.

How was it that I was always the last one to know about these things?! "Yes. That Change."

"Well, sure I do. I'm a doorman."

"And is it really, really bad?" I asked anxiously.

"It can be," I heard a familiar voice say behind me.

I jumped and turned around to see Blair standing there wearing a Lucky Charms T-shirt, crunching away on some pita chips. For someone who was kind of loud, he sure could sneak up without a sound. I wished he would wear a bell or something.

"You know Marc Whitby in 3E?" he asked. "The kid who goes to that special school in New Hampshire because he's a pyro?"

I shrugged. "I think I was in the elevator with him once." If it was the kid I was thinking of, he was really creepy. Like stringy-hair-talking-to-himself-under-his-breath creepy.

"Before his mother got remarried, he was at the top of his class at Horace Mann," Blair said. Horace Mann was one of the many different private schools in New York. "*And* captain of the soccer team. *And* the lacrosse team."

"He was?" When I saw him, he looked like he would've gotten winded just walking to the bathroom.

Blair nodded. "Yup. Rumor has it that when The Change happened, his mom stopped coming to all his games because she was too busy going to watch his stepsister ride horses."

I knew his stepsister. She was this annoying girl named Taylor who was obsessed with all things horses and was in all these equestrian competitions. In fact, with her long face and buck teeth, she kind of looked like a horse.

"It was like as soon as the ink was dry on the marriage license, Marc just became ... *invisible*," Blair said.

I felt my stomach start to get wonky—was that what was going to happen? Sure, up until now Mom and Alan had done a good job at making me feel like I was just as important as Laurel even though I wasn't famous. Was that all just an act? After things were officially official, was everyone going to start ignoring me? Laurel was already Miss Piggy's favorite—was she going to become both Mom and Alan's, too? I was so freaked out I couldn't even think about the fact that yet again he hadn't brought up getting together.

Just then my phone beeped with a text from Alan. *LUCY—PLEASE REPORT TO THE LIVING ROOM ASAP FOR AN EMERGENCY FAMILY MEETING. THANK YOU.* Uh-oh. All caps was never good, especially when they came from Alan.

OK, I texted back. *Did you tell Laurel yet?*

SHE'S ALREADY HERE, he wrote back.

That meant he had told her about the meeting first. If we were *equal*, he would've texted us both at the same time.

This was not good.

This meeting had a special guest star—Laurel's publicist, Marci.

"Oh hiiiii, Lisa!" Marci said all fakely from the living room couch. According to Laurel, most everything about Marci was fake: her hair color, her nails ... even her boobs. Just like when I had met her in Los Angeles, her shiny red hair was perfectly combed and she was wearing super-high heels. Even though she lived in L.A. and not New York City, she was dressed in all black, which, according to Pete, was the New Yorker's uniform. (You only had to look at Beatrice to know that was true.)

"It's Lucy," I corrected. "Lisa" was what all the gossip columns had called me when they thought I was dating Connor Forrester.

"Oh right. Sorry," she replied, flashing a very white smile. "Look at how ... *colorful* you are." She tried to make her voice sound like she thought that was a good thing, but I could tell from the way she cringed that she was anti-color. Which meant that she was anti-me because I was all about color and a big supporter of wearing as many different ones as possible at once. For instance, in the form of a purple corduroy miniskirt with a red angora sweater and rainbow tights and lilac Converse sneakers, like I was right then.

Picking up the gavel that Mom had bought him as a jokey anniversary gift but that he took very seriously, Alan pounded it on the coffee table. "I hereby call this Parker-Moses Family Meeting to order!" he called out. "Laurel, sweetie, can you sit up straight and look a little less blind?" he asked. "I know you're just preparing for your role, but because you're so good at it, it makes me nervous."

She smiled. "You really think I look blind?"

"Very much so, honey," Mom agreed with a smile.

A smile. Huh. That was very Change-like. Because the last conversation *I* had with Mom she hadn't been smiling. She had been frowning—as she said, "Lucy Beth Parker, if you bring up that kitten idea one more time, I'm going to take away your DVR privileges. End of story." (The use of my middle name was never good. And when paired with "end of story"? Even worse.)

"Oh totally," said Marci. "Like I keep saying . . . hello, Academy Award!"

"An interesting opportunity has come up, but because it's something that would affect the whole family, I wanted us to discuss it all together," Alan said. "And now I turn the floor over to Marci. Please hold your questions until she's finished." He held out the gavel. "Would you like this?"

"I think I'm okay," she replied. She flashed us another one of her white smiles. "Okay, so yesterday, I came up with this very, *very* cool idea." Things were always "very, *very*" in Marci's world. Usually very, *very* cool or very, *very* uncool. "Okay, so Laurel? Even though you haven't started shooting the movie yet and Oscar nominations won't be announced until a year from January, it's very, *very* important that we get started on your campaign, like, *immediately*. And while I know that it's always been

40

very, *very* important to you to keep your personal and home life personal and...*home life-like*, I got to thinking that it could be very, *very* cool if you did a *Week with Wendi*.

When she heard that, Laurel didn't look blind—she looked like she was about to die.

"You know, so that when Academy voters go to vote, they'll remember seeing the show and feel as if they really know you as a person," Marci went on.

Mom and Alan looked at each other. While Alan had one of his hopeful doesn't-that-sound-GREAT? smiles on, Mom's was more like I-think-I-just-ate-a-piece-of-bad-sushi. "So what you're saying is that you want us to let this woman into our home and spend a week following us around?" she asked.

Even though Marci shook her head hard, her hair barely moved. "No, no, *no!*" she cried.

The color returned to Mom's face. "Oh. Okay. So she's just going to tape Laurel at the studio?"

"No. What I meant is that she'd follow the family around for *three* weeks!" Marci replied. "From now through the wedding!"

Now it was Laurel who looked like she was going to throw up. "Look, I know that there's a few people out there who are interested in my life"—A *few*?! There were so many people interested that last time I Googled her, I counted 328 unofficial Laurel Moses websites—"but I highly doubt that if you asked Wendi Wallerstein if she wanted to spend three weeks following me around, she'd say yes."

"Actually, I did ask her—well, I asked her executive producer, Camilla—and Wendi called me back *herself* while in the middle of her private Pilates session and said that she'd be *honored* to follow you and your family around before this monumental event."

"I really don't know why people are making such a big deal about this wedding," Mom said with a nervous laugh. "In fact, it's not even a wedding. It's more like ... a small gathering of our immediate family. And I can tell you right now—I think that following us around would be of very little interest to a TV audience." Mom was a very private person. So private that she wouldn't even watch any sort of reality show just out of principle because she thought that the fact that TV made celebrities out of regular people was not a good thing. She wouldn't even watch *Hoarders*, which, if you asked me, was a total loss on her part because that show was the most awesome of all the reality shows.

Marci shrugged. "Small gathering, monumental event—same thing. *Any*way," she continued, "you know I don't like to tell you what to do, Laurel, but as your publicist, with three years of top-notch experience at *the* hottest PR firm in all of Hollywood, I strongly believe you should do this."

Laurel sighed. The only thing she wanted more than the NeatDesk, this digital filing scanner system we had seen advertised on TV one night, was an Oscar. She shook her head. "I don't know. This is my family we're talking about."

One of the coolest things about Laurel was that while she accepted the fact that because she was so famous, there was a certain amount of living in the public eye she had to do, she tried to do that only when she was at work on her TV show or a movie or at a special event. When she was with us, her family, she was super low-key. And if we were all out, she wore a hat and sunglasses or a full-on disguise. We weren't one of those families where everyone became famous just because we were the Frister or Parents Of the famous person. ("I'm still waiting for someone to tell me what exactly those Kardashian people have done to make them famous," Mom was always saying.) We were just . . . normal. Well, normal other than the fact that we had a lot of family meetings and a binder full of official rules and regulations.

Laurel turned to us. "What do you guys think?"

"I'd be okay with it," I piped up. "Well, I'd be okay with it as long as Wendi didn't come into my room on the days when it wasn't clean." Which, pretty much, was all days other than the first hour after Mom had forced me to clean it. While *I* didn't have a problem with things not being in their proper drawers, some people in America did.

Marci nodded. "I could totally put that in the contract, Lisa."

"It's *Lucy*," Laurel corrected her.

"And I'm sure people would be very interested in seeing what went on during a well-run family meeting," Alan added. "Who knows—maybe it would help other families get organized!"

Or, maybe when that part came on, they'd take a bathroom or snack break.

Still, Mom looked doubtful. And Laurel could tell. She shook her head. "I don't think it's a good idea. The movie is important, but it's not, like, *everything* to me."

Because of the actress thing, Laurel was an excellent liar. But even someone who barely had any experience lying—like a nun or a priest—would have done a better job than she was right then.

"Laurel, you spend every moment that you're not sleeping practicing your lines and pretending to be blind," I said. "And, on the nights you wear your earphones and listen to the script on your iPod as you fall asleep, you're even rehearsing in your *sleep*."

"Okay, fine. So maybe this movie is the best role that's ever been offered to me," she admitted.

"Did I mention that the last four Best Actress winners all did a *Week with Wendi* at some point before they won?" Marci interrupted. "Because they did."

"But, still," Laurel went on, "having a camera crew follow you around for three weeks is a big deal. And I totally respect the fact that some people don't like reality TV."

She made sure not to look at Mom when she said that, but it was obvious that's who she was talking about because none of us had problems with it. Even Alan liked watching reality TV. Especially the shows where someone went in and organized a person's life after totally shaming them for being such a mess.

As respectful as Laurel was being, and as nice as my mother was, I knew my mom well enough to know that there was no way she would say yes to this. And I also knew her well enough to know that there'd be something about how the people who let their lives be televised were seriously hurting their karma.

She sighed. "It's okay. I guess I could handle it for a few weeks."

Wait a minute. Backspace. *What*? Who just said that? That was not my mother.

"Really? Are you sure?" Laurel asked anxiously.

"Honey, if you don't want to do it, it's completely okay," Alan said.

Mom shrugged. "No, it's fine." She looked at Laurel and smiled. "I know what this would mean to Laurel."

Another smile? It looked like Marissa was right. The wedding may not have happened yet, but already The Change was.

Laurel squealed and threw her arms around Mom's neck, almost pushing her over. "But I just have one request," Mom managed to get out.

"Anything!" Laurel squealed.

Mom looked at Marci. "I want Wendi focusing primarily on Laurel. *Not* the small gathering with immediate family that's going to take place in a few weeks."

"You mean the wedding," Alan said.

Mom started to scratch at the inside of her left wrist, something that happened when she got nervous about something. "*No*, I mean the *small gathering of immediate family*. End of story."

I watched as she itched some more.

"Faaaaabuuuulous," purred Marci as she took out her cell phone. "I'll let Wendi's people know.

"So when would they start?" I asked, yanking at the ends of my hair in an attempt to make it grow faster so it looked long on camera.

"Probably tomorrow," Marci replied.

At that, Mom didn't look like she ate just one piece of bad sushi, but an entire meal.

chapter 3

Dear Dr. Maude,

You may have already heard the big news because Pete says that Mrs. Weinstein from 11F (I'm sure you know her—she's one of the biggest gossips in the building) is blabbing on about it to whoever will listen and trying to call an emergency co-op board meeting to stop it. But if you haven't, Wendi Wallerstein is doing a *Week with Wendi* based on Laurel! And because we live with Laurel, it's based on our entire family. But in our case it's not just a week—it's THREE weeks because they're going follow us through the wedding.

The wedding I'm referring to is the one that's going to happen between Alan and Mom in less than a month. I mentioned it in a previous e-mail but because I'm not sure you READ my e-mails, I thought I'd bring it up again. Although according to my mom, we're not allowed to call it a wedding. It's a "small gathering of immediate family."

I'm not sure what's going on with her. I know because she's a feminist, she's not the type of woman to get all crazy about a wedding and talk about what kind of pots and pans she's going to ask people to get her as gifts and wear a dress that makes her look like a meringue (BTW—do you like meringues? I used to not like them, but now I do.) But still, every time someone brings it up—ESPECIALLY if they call it a wedding rather than a small gathering of immediate family—she gets all huffy and says, "Can we please change the subject?" And then if someone says, "Fine. I have a subject we can change it to: how about we talk about how nice it would be to hear the patter of small kitten feet around the apartment?" she gets even huffier.

Oh—BTW—I was wondering. Are YOU a feminist? Because I'm still not entirely sure what feminism exactly is, I'm not sure if I'm one. I think I am, though. Do you have any idea how old you have to be before you can be one? I guess I could always Google it, but I thought if you knew it would save me some time. Well, except for the fact that you never write me back so waiting for you to get back to me with an answer would probably be a waste of time rather than a time-saver.

Well, I should get going. Mom's making me clean my room extra good before school because Wendi and her crew are coming this afternoon. I'm actually excited about being on TV. Not because I'm full of myself like Cristina Pollock, but because I feel like it will be a good opportunity for me to show the world that you can be non-famous and live with someone famous and still lead a happy life. Plus, there might be opportunities for me to pass along some of my advice to a larger audience than just the kids who read the newspaper at the Center for Creative Learning. (I told you that I'm no longer going by "Annie" to keep my identity a secret, right? But don't worry—it's not like I'm trying to compete with you for business or anything like that).

Okay, well, bye!

yours truly,
LUCY B. PARKER

P.S. If you have a chance to get back to me with some advice about what to do about people who get all snippy about their own weddings, I'd appreciate it. Thanks. Bye.

"Can I can come over after school today?" Alice asked at lunch later. "I think I left my rhinestone barrette in your room last time I was there."

"You did, but I gave it back to you the next day, remember?" I replied.

"Oh right," she said, disappointed.

"Plus, Wendi Wallerstein is coming over to go over everything so I can't hang out."

Alice gave a (very fake) gasp. "Omigod—she *is*? I didn't know that!"

Even Malia—the nicest person in the world—let out a sigh.

Beatrice rolled her eyes. "Yes, you did. You spent most of science class saying, 'Omigod, I can't believe my

Wendi Wallerstein is doing an entire show about my best friend!'"

"I did?" Alice said. "Well, I guess I keep forgetting."

"The show really isn't about me," I corrected, "it's about Laurel." I left out "and, Alice, while you're a good friend of mine, you're not my best friend" because I didn't want to hurt her feelings.

Alice smacked her forehead. "Oh no! You know what?"

"What, Alice?" I asked.

"Remember how last time I was there we snuck those rice cakes in your room?"

I nodded.

"Well, I think I left the crumpled-up package on your desk instead of throwing it in the garbage," she said. "So I should probably check. I don't want you to get ants or anything. Especially because I know that one of the Parker-Moses official rules is 'No eating outside of the kitchen' for *exactly* that reason."

Like Marissa, Alice was obsessed with trying to become famous. Unfortunately, for her, all five blogs she had started had no followers other than me, Beatrice, Malia, and Marissa (even though they had never met, they had agreed to link to each other's blogs in order to try to get more traffic. Which, because no one other than us was following them, didn't work.). And because we were also her only followers on the three different Twitter accounts she had, she wasn't becoming famous that way, either.

"Alice, I keep telling you, according to Laurel, being famous isn't all that great," I said. "You know, other than those fancy loot bags you get at special events and the gift baskets full of cookies and brownies and cupcakes around the holidays."

"Well, if I can't be on the TV special, can I at least come to the wed—small gathering of immediate family?" she asked. "I just *love* wed—small gatherings of immediate family. I already have a dress picked out. It's so pretty. It's blue with—"

"Alice, are you part of Lucy's immediate family?" Beatrice demanded.

The fact that Alice actually took a second to think about it made me really wonder about whether or not her brain had been knocked loose when she fell off a horse at camp this past summer.

Before she could reply, Roger Friedman, this kid in our grade wearing a T-shirt that looked like a tuxedo top and high-waisted jeans, walked up.

"Hey, Lucy!" he exclaimed. Roger was big on the exclaiming front. Because Alice was, too, Beatrice kept trying to convince her to use him as her local crush instead of Max Rummel, seeing that she had been crushing/stalking Max since second grade and it hadn't worked yet. But Alice refused, saying that she was worried about hurting Max's feelings if she gave him up.

"Hey, Roger," I said.

"So I know in the paper it says if I want advice, I

should ask you. It says I'm supposed to send all questions via e-mail but I was wondering if just this once you might be able to answer it this way," he said. "Because it's something I kind of need an answer on right away."

I shrugged. "Okay."

"Hold on a second!" Beatrice ordered. "If we do that for you, we're going to have to do that for everyone. Guidelines are guidelines for a *reason*."

I loved Beatrice, but she could be kind of bossy. Although Alan would've approved of what she was saying. "I think it's okay this one time," I said.

"Really?! That's *great!*" Roger exclaimed. "Okay, so here's my question. See, there's this girl—"

"You should really save this for the special crush edition of the advice column," Beatrice interrupted. "We're targeting it for the third week of January."

Correction: Beatrice could be *very* bossy.

"It's not about a crush," Roger replied. "As I was saying, there's this girl, and I'd really like her to invite me over to her house but I don't want it to *seem* like I'm trying to get her to invite me over to her house because I don't want her to think that I'm using her or anything. So how do I do that?"

"Why do you want to go to her house?"

"Because this famous TV host is going to be there and I want to meet her because I feel like if I'm on TV, I might be able to get a record deal for my harmonica playing."

Roger was the president of the Harmonica Harmoners club at our school. ("Is Harmoners even a *word*?" Beatrice had asked the other day.) Seeing that he was the only member, he was also the vice president and secretary as well.

"So what you're asking for is advice on how to get me to invite you over so you can meet Wendi and be discovered and become a big star?"

He looked confused. "How'd you know that?!" he exclaimed.

I sighed. I was starting to question what I was getting myself into.

Wendi Wallerstein didn't talk. She chirped. Like a bird. Not only did she chirp, but she also hopped around like one, with tiny birdlike feet that were inside high, high heels.

"Gang, all of us at *Week with Wendi*—especially *moi*—are just sooooo excited and honored about sharing your lives for the next three weeks!" she chirped later that afternoon. Camilla, her executive producer; Nikko, the cameraman; and Siouxsie, the makeup woman, didn't look all that excited. In fact, they looked pretty bored. The only one paying attention was her assistant, Charles. As Wendi hopped around the living room examining our framed photos and books, she reminded me of one of the detectives in those *Law & Order* shows that Beatrice liked to watch. That is, if the detectives wore Pepto Bismol–pink skirts and blazers.

As Wendi took one of Dad's framed photographs from his and Sarah's trip to India the year before off the wall and started to examine it, I watched Mom cringe. "I'd really you rather not—"

Before she could finish, Wendi dropped the photo and the sound of breaking glass could be heard.

"—touch those," Mom finished.

"Whoops. Sorry about that. My nails are still a little wet so I don't want to smudge them."

I could tell that it was taking everything in Mom to not say something like, "Hey, who do you think you are going through our personal things like that?"

Wendi hopped over to a chair and settled herself in it. "So. Before we start shooting, I just wanted to go over a few guidelines," she chirped. She pointed at Charles ("It's spelled that boring old regular way, but it's pronounced *Sharles*, with an S-h," he sniffed after I made the mistake of pronouncing it the boring old regular C-h way) and snapped her fingers. "Charles! Charles! Guidelines!"

Laurel turned to me and gave me a look. Well, what I was pretty sure would've been a look if I could see her eyes through her dark glasses. In order to show Wendi how committed she was to her acting, she had decided to stay in character the whole time. Complete with tapping her cane as she walked and occasionally bumping into walls.

She thrust the pages to Alan. "Here you go, honey. Just take a look at this at your leisure—or have your attorney go over them, however you like to handle these things—and then get it back to Camilla."

Alan began to flip through them. "*Guests will answer personal questions as honestly as possible*," he read. "*If said guest begins to cry because Wendi has asked a very deep personal question, said guest will not attempt to stop aforementioned crying*."

"Just how deep and personal are we talking about here?" Mom asked warily.

"Oh, nothing out of the ordinary," Camilla replied. "Just, you know, memories of traumatic childhood events, that kind of stuff. Oh, and in this case, with the wedding coming up, any sort of fears that might be coming up about committing yourself to one person *for the rest of your life*."

At the w-word, Mom started scratching the inside of her wrist again. "We choose not to use the word 'wedding,'" she corrected. "It's a small intimate gathering of immediate family."

"Huh. Okay. But that's a very long-winded way of saying 'wedding,' don't you think?" Wendi asked. She turned to Charles. "I'm never going to remember that. Write that down."

"Ms. Wallerstein—" Mom began.

"Oh, honey, what's with this Ms. stuff—it's *Wendi*, sweetie!" she chirped.

"Okay, *Wendi*," Mom said. She gave her best fake smile, which, because Mom hated fakeness, wasn't very good. "Now I fully understand that part of the success of your show has to do with the way that you—"

"—are able to make her guests get to a deep emotional place that they're usually only able to get to after years in therapy?" Camilla suggested. "Which accounts for our last four Emmy awards?"

"Well, I guess that's one way of putting it," Mom said. "And while I'm sure some people find the idea of having that happen on national television very healing, our family is a little more ... *private* about that stuff."

"Oh, I *completely* get that, honey!" Wendi chirped. "I'm a very private person myself."

Laurel tapped me on my leg with her cane. "If she's so private, how come she's written three books about herself?" she whispered.

I shrugged. I hadn't read them, but apparently *Wendi!: The Early Years, Wendi!: The Late Early Years,* and *Wendi!: The Early Middle Years* had all been big bestsellers.

"It's just that research has found that the reason my show has consistently been the top-rated interview show on television for the last three seasons is because viewers consider me the perfect best friend," Wendi said.

I'm sorry, but if she was a middle schooler instead of however old she was (it was hard to tell on account of the fact that her face was very plastic-looking), she'd have as much trouble as Marissa did finding a best friend. And when she did, it would be someone equally annoying as that Cass girl.

"And when I'm with my guests, because I'm so best friend–like, they end up feeling safe enough to open up and confide in me and really let their hair down."

I reached back and grabbed a hunk of my own hair. I knew I had been looking forward to America seeing how long my hair had gotten, but suddenly I thought it might be safer to wear one of the many hats from my hat collection every time I was on camera so that this letting-my-hair-down thing didn't happen.

She turned to me. "Like, say, *you* . . . I'm sorry, what's your name again?"

"*Lucy*, Lucy B. Parker."

"Right. Right." She snapped at Charles again. "Charles, write that down. I'm never going to remember that." She turned back to me and smiled. "I want to know how it feels to live with the most famous girl in the world. I mean, that *can't* be easy."

I shrugged. "Actually, it is." Other than when she would sneak into my room and wipe down my blinds. That was annoying, but I wasn't going to embarrass her by bringing that up.

Her right eyebrow went up. "Really. Well, we'll see about that."

She turned to Laurel and smiled. "And Laurel, as someone who is obviously so committed to her art—"

Laurel beamed and moved her cane around a bit.

"—it must be difficult, being surrounded by so many ... how do I put this ... *non-creative* people—"

At that, the anxious smile that had been frozen on Alan's face shriveled up like Miss Piggy's head when I tried to pet her. "Excuse me, just because we're not performers doesn't mean we're not creative. This isn't something I advertise, but I'll have you know I write poetry."

Mom turned to him, surprised. "You do? I didn't know that."

"See what I mean about my ability to draw things out of people?" Wendi announced.

"I do. In fact, I'm working on something right now to read at the wed"—At Mom's look, he stopped himself—"small intimate gathering of immediate family."

I turned to Wendi. "And I get to give the toast," I said. "Because I'm class president, I've got a lot of public-speaking experience now and—"

"Fascinating," Wendi said, cutting me off before turning back to Laurel. "So, Laurel, as I was saying, how does it feel to be a creative person in a non-creative world?"

That was so not okay for her to treat me like I was some annoying little kid. And what was *also* not okay was the fact that Laurel didn't stick up for me and tell Wendi that. Instead she just sat there with what I had come to call her Superstar Smile (not fake, exactly, but very, very big and the kind that said, "There may be tons of people mobbing me at this moment, but as far as I'm concerned you're the only person in this room and all my attention is on you and if I were a regular person instead of a ginormous star, then we'd totally hang out *all* the time").

Before I could open my mouth to say, "Who says the rest of us aren't creative?!" Laurel got hers open first. "Well, Wendi, as an artist, I try and use real life as the basis for my work—"

Oh, now she wasn't even an actress, but an *artist?* Laurel hated when actors called themselves artists. She called it "pretentious," which was a fancy word for stuck up.

"Now, in this case, for my new movie *Life Is What Happens When You're Making Other Plans*, I'll be playing a girl who's blind—"

"And you are *so* believeable I almost can't stand it!" Wendi cried.

"Oh, you're so sweet, thank you," Laurel said. "And if we were looking at that metaphorically, then it would be like the girl was cut off from her family—"

The rest of her family—meaning me, Mom, and Alan—looked at each other nervously.

"—which, obviously, in this situation, is not the case," Laurel continued. "Because my family does understand me. But in the case of my character in my new movie *Life Is What Happens When You're Making Other Plans*—"

I cringed. Why did I have the feeling that this whole thing was going to be one giant ad for Laurel's new movie?

"—she doesn't feel understood. And the blindness—the blindness just *externalizes* her *internal* conflict."

"It sounds like such a *meaty* role," Wendi chirped.

"Oh, it is," Laurel agreed.

"Well, I am *so* looking forward hearing more about it," Wendi chirped as she stood up and smoothed her skirt. "But right now, before I leave, I think we need a big group hug!"

As for me, what I needed was to disappear into my room and watch today's episode of Dr. Maude's show, *Come On, People—Get with the Program.*

"Come on, come on!" she squealed when no one got up. She looked over at Nikko. "Is the camera on? Turn it on and get this on tape," she ordered.

After we didn't move, she *click-clacked* over in her high heels and threw her arms around us, smooshing us together. For someone so little, she sure was strong. "Hug, gang! *Hug!*"

"Ufff," I said as the hug got tighter and my nose ended up somewhere near Mom's armpit. Luckily, she had remembered to put on deodorant that morning.

"*This* is what I'm talking about!" Wendi chirped, close to my right ear. "Nikko, are you getting this?"

"I'm getting this," he replied in a bored voice.

"Make sure you get my right side. You *know* that's my better side."

"I'm getting your right side," he said, just as bored.

"Okay, enough of the hugging," she said as she let go and we all ricocheted back like slingshots. "Wasn't that nice? Don't you all just feel warm and fuzzy and sooo much closer?" Before we could respond, she clapped her hands. "We're going to have so much fun together over the next few weeks!".

I didn't have to look over at Mom to know that she kind of thought differently.

chapter 4

Dear Dr. Maude,

I was wondering whether you've heard about The Change. And I'm not talking about the "change of life," which is what kept coming up when I Googled "The Change." In case you didn't know, the "change of life" means menopause, which, when I Googled that, is what happens when you get really old and stop getting your period. But you probably already know that because (a) you're really smart and a doctor even though you're not a real doctor but only a shrink one and (b) you're old so for all I know that may have happened to you already. (Wait. That came out wrong. I didn't mean you were old-old. I just meant . . . You know what? Just forget that last part.)

The Change I'm talking about is the thing that happens after adults get remarried and start showing their true colors. Marissa told me about it. As I may have mentioned, you can't believe a lot of what Marissa says because she has what Dad calls an "overactive imagination" and tends to exaggerate. But when it comes to stuff having to do with divorce, you kind of can believe her. So I'm worried she might be right.

Anyway, without exactly knowing whether this Change

thing is real or just something that Marissa made up, I will say that there's definitely something weird going on. First of all, whenever anyone brings up the wedding—like Mrs. Chin at the cleaners—Mom starts to scratch the inside of her wrist, and even though she tries to sound all polite, you can hear her voice get all high as she tells people that she really doesn't understand why they're making a big deal about it because it's just a regular day like any other.

And then there's the way that Laurel's acting all star-like whenever Wendi and her crew are around. I know her new movie is really important to her because it's a great role that will show the world that she can do more than be Madison Tennyson, but, still, part of what was so great about Laurel was that she was so NOT starlike. But now, whenever Wendi and her crew are here she does stuff like flip her hair and laugh really loud at the things they say that're not all that funny.

I haven't mentioned this to anyone yet, but what if Laurel stays like this even after Wendi is gone? What if part of The Change is that all this time I've known Laurel, she's just been ACTING like she's a normal person when in fact she's REALLY this fake superstar? Because if that's the case, I'm not sure I can keep living with her. I really love my life in New York City, but if I'm going to feel like the unfamous, not-as-good-as little sister of the most famous girl of the world all the time, then I'd rather move back to Northampton and live with Dad and Sarah and Ziggy. Even if that means sleeping on an air mattress in the basement.

And if that happens, you and I won't be neighbors anymore, which would make me really sad. Not that being neighbors has mattered anyway. I mean, it's not like it made you answer any of my e-mails.

Thanks in advance for the advice you're finally going to give me about how to make things—and people, like Laurel and Mom—go back to normal.

yours truly,
LUCY B. PARKER

P.S. I think it's so awful that you stop getting your period when you're old. Do you happen to know if there's anything to do to keep that from happening? Because even though I haven't gotten mine yet, I already know that I'm going to love it and want to have it forever.

"*Sisters,*" Wendi gasped dramatically the next afternoon as she paced around Laurel's bedroom while Laurel and I sat on the bed behind her. My back was killing me from sitting up so straight. Usually when Laurel and I hung out in her room, I sprawled out on the bed, sometimes in a giant backbend with my head hanging over the foot of it almost touching her floor. Having the entire world see that—especially if something happened and my shirt

flew up so everyone could see my bra—felt like a dangerous thing to do.

"Who else can you *laugh* with?" Wendi demanded as
she *click-clacked* across the room.

I glanced over at Laurel to maybe share a can-you-
believe-her? look, but Laurel was staring straight ahead
with her can't-you-tell-I'm-blind sunglasses and a movie-
star smile.

"*Cry* with," she went on.

I felt like crying right then and there. And if there
hadn't been a camera pointed at me, I probably would
have.

"And, of course . . . *shop* with?"

I snuck another look at Laurel, who was still blind,
and still smiling.

"To the world, superstar Laurel Moses has always
seemed to lead a charmed life. Award-winning television
and film star. Grammy-nominated singer. Over *two
million* followers on Twitter," she went on. "But behind
the gloss and glitz of Laurel's life was a *tragic secret*."

"There was?" I blurted out. I looked at Laurel,
confused. Here I was, thinking we had been BFFs all this
time, only to find out that obviously we were not. Because
BFFs did not keep tragic secrets from each other.

Wendi continued to slowly *click-clack* across the
room, so slowly that each *click* and each *clack* had an
almost hypnotizing-like feel. "Yes. There was," she went

on. "You see, what the world did not know was that Laurel was desperately. . . . *lonely*."

Laurel's face turned red. "I wouldn't say I was *lonely*."

"Of course you were," Wendi said as she *click-clacked* over and wedged herself between us on the bed. "But when your father, Alan, fell in love with Lucy Parker's—"

"Lucy *B.* Parker," I quickly corrected.

"—Lucy *B.* Parker's mother, Rebecca," she went on, "both of your lives were forever changed. And do you know *why* they were changed?"

"Because I had to move from Northampton, Massachusetts, to New York City?" I guessed.

"No. Because both of you finally knew the joy of having a sister. Someone you can tell your secrets to." Or, in mine and Laurel's case, *not* tell your secrets. "Someone you can—"

"Play The World's Ugliest Outfit with at the Holyoke Mall and then end up in the security office once everyone realizes that the girl wearing the yellow sequined top is the most famous girl in America?" I guessed.

"Well, I was going to say 'someone you can rely on,' but I guess that works, too," Wendi replied.

When I looked at Laurel, she was smiling. That had been a great day. Although Laurel had made us stop every two seconds so she could take pictures of things like the food court and the have-your-name-written-on-a-grain-of-rice necklace kiosk because she hadn't ever been to a regular mall. That had gotten tiring.

"We actually prefer the term 'frister,'" I said. "It's a combination of friend and sister."

"That is *so* cute!" Wendi squealed. "Laurel, you are very, *very* clever."

"Actually, it's *my* word," I piped up.

"Oh. Interesting," she said in a way that made it sound like because I was the one who had come up with it, it was suddenly a lot less interesting. She turned to me. "Lucy, I would really love it if you could let us in on what it's like to like to live with the most famous girl in America."

I forced myself to not roll my eyes. The last thing I needed was for people to write all sorts of stuff on message boards after the show aired about how I was jealous of Laurel. But if Wendi pointed out one more time that Laurel was famous and I wasn't, I was going to scream.

"It's . . . uh . . . interesting," I replied.

Laurel gave a tinkly laugh. Since when had she started to tinkle? "What does that mean, Lucy?" To the average person the question would've sounded normal, but because I knew Laurel so well, I could hear the nervousness underneath it.

"Interesting meaning . . . interesting," I said. It wasn't like I was going to tell all of America about the fact that she had went through a bottle of Purell a week. Although with the way she was acting, she kind of deserved it.

"Why don't you girls tell us about the first time you met," Wendi said. "Was it BFFdom at first sight?"

Laurel tinkled again. "Not exactly. In fact, it's a *very* funny story—"

My hands got clammy. "You know, Laurel, I doubt anyone wants to hear that story," I said, trying to sound equally tinkly. Unfortunately, when I did it, it sounded more like a donkey braying. I leaned in to Wendi. "It's kind of boring," I whispered.

"No, it isn't," Laurel said.

"Yes, it is," I said, giving her a look that said, Okay, Laurel, because we're fristers, I know you can hear what I'm thinking even though I'm not actually using my voice to say it. So since that's the case, you know what I'm thinking is that if you tell the story about the Hat Incident on national television, I will have to kill you.

Laurel smiled at the camera. "Lucy calls it the Hat Incident, which I think is *super* cute."

"Oh, that *is* super cute!" Wendi agreed.

This time I let my eyes roll. I bet if Laurel had said, "Pink is a really ugly color," Wendi would've said, "Omigod—*so* ugly!" even though it's all she ever wore.

Laurel went on to tell the story about the first day we met—in front of the Tattered Cover bookstore in Northampton when the director of the movie she was shooting grabbed the hat off my head, exposing the horrible haircut I had gotten after the Straightening Iron Incident that made me look like an egghead. I sat there with my fake smile, holding on to the blanket with both hands in order to stop myself from smothering Laurel with a pillow.

After she was done, she threw her arm around my shoulder and smiled at me. "And the rest is history, right, Lucy?"

I studied her face. Had she been trying to embarrass me with that story, or was she just totally clueless and really thought it was super cute? After a second, I decided she just thought it was a super cute. Which, frankly, was a little scary.

Wendi shook her head slowly. "*What* a beginning to a friendship." She turned to me. "Now Lucy," she said. "What would you say the biggest difference is between you and Laurel? You know, other than she's famous and you're not."

Laurel raised her hand. "Oh, I know one way!" she cried.

If Laurel was just a regular girl who went to regular school, she'd totally have a reputation for being a bit of a know-it-all.

Wendi smiled. "What is it?"

"Well, I'm a little on the neat side," she said. "Whereas Lucy...um...." She held up her hands and shrugged.

I turned to her. "What does *that* mean?"

"Nothing. Just that you're a little on the...*other* side," she replied.

"Are you saying that I'm on the *messy* side?" I

demanded. "We've talked about this before. I'm not messy," I said stubbornly. "I'm . . . *creatively organized.*"

Wendi nodded. "'*Creatively organized,*'" she said. "I like that."

I smiled. Score one for Lucy B. Parker. *Finally.* "Thanks. I came up with it the other day."

Laurel laughed. "I guess that's one way of putting it."

Okay, that was it. To tell embarrassing stories about your frister was one thing, but to accuse her of being messy *on national televsion*? That was crossing a line. My eyes narrowed. "At least I don't wipe down my blinds for fun. Or sneak into other people's rooms and wipe down *theirs.*"

If Dad were there, he'd tell me that a true Buddhist doesn't try to get back at someone by saying something mean to her, but (a) I wasn't sure if I wanted to be a Buddhist yet anyway and (b) between mentioning the Hat Incident *and* my creative organizing to the entire world, Laurel deserved a dose of her own medicine.

Laurel sat up straight and crossed her arms. "Dust is a silent killer," she replied. "There was an entire special about it on the Discovery Channel last week."

I couldn't believe she had just admitted she watched an entire program about *dust.* And not just to me but to the *world.* I didn't have to worry about embarrassing her—she had just done it herself.

"Yeah, well, a certain amount of dust is also healthy," I shot back. "It helps your immune system."

"Who told you that? Sarah?" Laurel asked.

"I can't remember," I replied. Okay, so maybe I hadn't exactly *heard* it. But even though I hadn't, I bet that someone, somewhere had once said it. "Plus, a little bit of unorganization is good for your brain." Maybe I hadn't exactly heard *that*, either, but I was even more sure of that one than the dust-being-healthy one. "It makes it ... work harder."

She laughed. "I guess we have different ideas of a 'little' and 'a lot.'"

"I guess we do," I tinkled as I smiled for the camera.

As Wendi continued the interview and Laurel and I pretended that nothing was wrong even though, because we knew each other so well, we both knew something was wrong, I thought about how it now seemed like we had different ideas about a lot of things.

That night, after Wendi and her crew left, for the first time since it had come on the air, Laurel and I didn't watch *The Real Ghost Housewives of Des Moines* together. Usually we crawled into her bed together (not surprisingly, she didn't like watching in my room ... probably because of the invisible dust that apparently really bothered her even though she had never actually told me that). During the really scary parts (and there were many because some of those housewives were *mad*) we'd grab onto each other. But that night I was forced to watch it by myself. At first I tried to make Miss Piggy watch it with me by locking her in my room, but being hissed at isn't much fun—especially when you're already scared. I tried to ignore the fact that once I let her out, she ran straight for Laurel's room and pawed at the door until Laurel opened it (it took her a few tries because of the blind thing).

After the show was over I decided to do some brainstorming about how to make things go back to the way they used to be. Taking out my favorite purple marker and my notebook that was titled "Miscellaneous Lists and Other List-Like Things" (there weren't actually any other list-like things in it, but to use Wite-Out to take that off the cover would've made it look ugly), I turned to a clean page and wrote "Things to Do to Make Things Go Back to How They Were Pre-Change aka Before Everyone in My Family ESPECIALLY My Mom and Laurel Started Acting All Weird)."

1. Invent a time machine in order to turn back time. Which isn't going to happen because (a) I'm not an inventor-type person and (b) that only happens in movies and children's books.

2. Follow Rule #7 of the Official Parker-Moses Family Rule Book, which states, "All family members must try to resolve any and all conflict that arises within the family so that it does not turn into a resentment." But that's not going to work because that would mean going into Laurel's room and saying I wanted to talk to her, which she would take to mean I was there to APOLOGIZE, which I AM NOT because I DIDN'T DO ANYTHING WRONG.

3. Try that praying thing again because back when I was scared to tell Beatrice about my crush on Blair and I did it, it kind of worked. But from what I had heard, you can't really control when you receive an answer to your prayer and I need one immediately.

4. Write Dr. Maude an e-mail asking for advice. Also not going to work—see #3 for why.

5. Get into bed and go to sleep and hope that things will be better in the morning.

I looked at the list and realized that nothing I had come up with so far seemed all that inspired, so I decided it was time to step things up. Which, in this case, meant doing a headstand. According to Alice, doing headstands helped you come up with answers to problems. ("Something about the blood leaving your brain or the dizziness when you stand up.") The whole thing sounded pretty fishy to me, but because (a) I was out of ideas and (b) I wanted to see if by any chance my coordination had improved at all, I decided to give it a try.

When you're a person with coordination issues, getting up into a headstand takes a few tries. Like, say, five. It also results in your mother standing outside your door demanding, "Lucy Beth Parker, *what* is going on in there?!" and you saying, "Nothing. Just trying to practice doing a headstand," and her replying, "Your bedroom is not a yoga studio so unless you can do it away from the wall like Laurel, save it for gym class." (One thing I had noticed post-Change was that Mom compared me to Laurel more than usual. And *not* in a good way but more like pointing out things that Laurel was better at than me.)

Finally, I made it up. But once there, I wasn't sure what to do—did I think about my problem and hope that the answer came to mind while I was up there? Did I *not* think about my problem? Did I try not to get grossed out by the dust bunnies under my bed that I could now see and worry that maybe Laurel was right and if we ever made up, I should let her move my bed and sweep under there like she was always begging to do? Did I worry about what my life would be like if I broke my neck while in the headstand and became a paraplegic? (I wondered if that happened, if Laurel would want to play me in the movie version.) After what seemed like about a half hour but, when I looked at my bedside clock, was only more like two minutes, I came down. Not only solutionless, but with a crick in my neck.

"So much for that," I sighed as I stood up and cringed at the heel prints I had left on my purple walls. Although there was nothing in the Parker-Moses Family Rules Book that stated, "No heel prints on walls," I had a feeling that, in Alan's eyes, it was almost as a bad as sneaking food into the bedroom. But then—as I walked over to my desk to make a new list titled "Things NOT to Do to

Make Things Go Back to How They Were Pre-Change" where number one would be *Do a headstand to help with brainstorming for an answer*—it hit me.

I would come up with the best, most fantastic, unbelievably awesome wedding toast ever. It would be a video and when everyone saw it, Mom would be so impressed that she'd go back to being normal, and Wendi would see that Laurel wasn't the only talented, creative person in the family.

And I would ask Blair to help me because he was the ex-president of the AV club.

Although I preferred the idea of asking Blair via e-mail—especially because I had dots of zit cream on my face—I decided that asking someone for such a big favor for nothing other than payment in fried Oreos (that was what I had paid him in when he did the video for my class president election) meant I should probably do it in person.

After washing off the zit cream and changing out of Mom's holey Smith sweatshirt into my new Woodstock Animal Sanctuary one (we had gone there for a field trip a few weeks before and other than the fact that I got stuck sitting next to Mallory Sullivan on the bus, who, apparently, was not familiar with the word "deodorant," it was an awesome day), I took the elevator down to Beatrice and Blair's apartment on the tenth floor.

Well, first I stopped on the twelfth floor, which was where Dr. Maude lived. Pete was always telling me that stalking other residents was "severely frowned upon" by the co-op board (that was the group of snooty adults who were in charge of saying who could move into the building, and whether or not people could leave their bikes in the basement), especially since he was the person who had originally let it slip that she lived there. But after I explained to him that it wasn't stalking unless you actually went up to the person's door and put your ear to it to see if you could hear whether or not they were home, he let it go.

Because what I was doing was not stalking. I just pushed the button in the elevator so that the door just *happened* to open on her floor, which allowed me to *possibly* run into her if she was coming out of her door at that moment. That was more like attempting to get to know my neighbors because I'm a very friendly person. Well, except when it comes to crazy people on the subway who mutter to themselves about how that morning as they were eating a hardboiled egg, the egg turned into a goblin and whispered that the world was going to end in six days and thirty-two hours. In that case, I just stared at the ground like all the other passengers with a don't-even-THINK-about-talking-to-me look on my face.

As usual, when the elevator doors opened, there was no sign of Dr. Maude. There was, however, a sign of what

I was pretty sure was Dr. Maude's umbrella (black, with a real wooden handle, which made me think it was kind of expensive as opposed to the small ones you could buy on the street for five bucks—seven, if it were particularly rainy—that always blew inside out and almost took your eye out before you had even made it down the block). Not only that, but there were two pairs of dog booties—one pink, one blue—neatly lined up next to it. I knew they belonged to her dachshunds, Id and Ego, and was a little tempted to go knock on the door and, if she answered, tell her that usually I found dog booties to be pretty silly looking, but in this case they were super cute. But because that came somewhat close to stalking, I stopped myself and let the doors close and continued down to the tenth floor.

When Beatrice opened the door, she was holding a yellow highlighter. "Here you go," she said, thrusting it out to me. I had decided that while it was a little bit of a stretch (i.e., somewhat close to a lie) for me to text Beatrice and ask if she had a yellow highlighter I could borrow, and if so, could I come down to her place and get it, it wouldn't affect my karma too much.

"Thanks," I said, taking it.

"But why didn't you ask Laurel for one?" she asked. "She's got an entire desk drawer of them."

That was true. Not only that, but they were all lined up perfectly. "Because we're kind-of, sort-of in a fight," I replied. I wasn't sure if that was entirely true, but to find out would have meant asking Laurel, and I didn't want to do that.

"Oh. Okay. Well, I'll see you in the morning," she said as she started to close the door.

I put my foot out to stop it. "Wait!" I cried.

She opened it. "What?" she asked impatiently. "*Pageant Queens Rehab* is on."

Pageant Queens Rehab was Beatrice's favorite show. The rehab that they sent the girls to wasn't for drugs but for makeup and diet food and hairspray. Basically, they got them off all that stuff and turned them into normal people again. Usually, Beatrice only liked documentaries about chimps in Africa or travel shows about Paris (she was planning on moving there when she grew up and becoming a famous writer), but after Alice forced us to watch it one night when we were having a sleepover at her house ("I know you guys are guests and all, but because it's my house I get to pick what we watch on TV") Beatrice was hooked. I found the way the women all looked like dolls with big blue eyes and spider-like eyelashes kind of creepy, but because I was a huge *Hoarders* fan, I wasn't in any position to judge.

"Okay, okay. I just . . . need to use your bathroom," I said. In an effort to look somewhat believable, I crossed my legs. And then added a hop and a wince. It would've made things so much easier if I felt more comfortable about having a crush on my best friend's brother.

She narrowed her eyes. "Where's your zit cream?" she demanded.

"Huh?"

"You always put your zit cream on at seven thirty."

Whoops. That was the problem with having a best friend who knew everything about you. "I, um ... see, the thing is—" I mumbled.

She cocked her head. "Ohhhh. I get it. You're here to see *him*." She gave me a look of utter disappointment. Much like Miss Piggy did when I walked toward her with my arms open so we could spend some quality bonding time together and she ran to the nearest small space where it was impossible for me to get to her. "He's in his room," she said as she padded back to the couch.

"It's a business thing," I called after her. "Not, like, you know, a *crush* thing."

"Whatever," she said.

I tried to think of something else to say to help my case, but I figured it was easier to just let her go back and watch her show. When I walked over to Blair's room, the door was closed and there was some sort of weird music playing. It was one thing to show up at someone's apartment to ask them something, but it was another to knock on their *closed door* behind which they were doing who knew what. Which is why I did what any normal person in my situation would do: I went and waited in the bathroom for him to come out.

Luckily, I didn't have to wait too long. About two

minutes later, my overlistening skills allowed me to hear the click of his door as it started to open. After waiting what felt like the right amount of time so that when I opened the door it would seem like I just *happened* to run into him, in his own house, at eight o'clock on a school night, I opened the door. And smacked him right in the face with it.

"OW!" he screeched after his nose bounced off it like one of those silver metal balls in a pinball game.

"I'm so sorry!" I cried. I wasn't sure what to do. In movies when that kind of thing happened, the unhurt person tended to the hurt person by checking to see if anything was broken. But because that would mean actually touching him, I hung back and just stood there as he jumped around from foot to foot like some sort of oversize *Zombie High* T-shirt-wearing leprechaun holding his nose saying, "Owowowowowow." Finally, he stopped and uncupped his nose. "Is it broken?" he demanded.

I leaned in and looked at it, but I wasn't sure what I was supposed to be looking for. Blood? A piece of bone sticking out? "How am I supposed to tell?"

"I don't know! Is it swollen?"

I shrugged. "I can't tell. It's as big as it always is." The minute the words left my mouth I realized that probably wasn't the best thing to say to either someone you had a crush on, or someone you were going to attempt to hire to help you make a kick-butt video toast so that America would find out you, too, had some talent. Or, in my case, both.

"Well, touch it and see if it's squishy."

I cringed. "You want me to . . . touch your nose?"

"Yes! I'd do it, but I'm in so much pain I think my neural transmitters are all screwed up."

I wasn't sure what a neural transmitter was, but it sounded pretty serious. I really hoped (a) they weren't screwed up, and (b) if they were, he didn't sue me because I was probably going to end up using the last of my savings to pay him in fried Oreos. It felt weird to be touching the nose of a boy you hadn't even kissed yet, but seeing that this was a medical emergency, I decided to go for it.

"OW!" he screeched again. "What are you doing?!"

"You told me to touch your nose!" I cried.

"I didn't tell you to press it so hard! If it wasn't already broken, it is now!" he yelled.

I took my finger away and stood back. "You know what? I think you should just touch it yourself, then," I shot back. This was not going well.

He did. Like from every angle. Once he had determined it wasn't broken ("Maybe seriously sprained," he said, "but probably not broken. Although we'll have to wait twenty-four hours to really know"), he turned to me. "So what are you doing here?" he asked. "I thought you didn't like *Pageant Queen Rehab*."

"I don't," I replied, making a mental note to Google

"What does it mean when a boy knows what TV shows you do and don't like" when I got back upstairs. "I'm actually here to see you."

It kind-of, sort-of looked like he turned a little red when I said that. It was a little difficult to tell because he was a bit sweaty from hopping around. "Oh yeah?"

I gave a half nod/half shrug. "Yeah."

"Why?" he demanded.

Jeez. Could he make this any harder for me? I wondered if I should find a crush who didn't make me feel like I was being grilled like a crime suspect in those SUV shows Beatrice liked to watch. ("It's *SVU*," she was always correcting me, "not *SUV*.") "I have a business proposition for you."

His eyes narrowed. "Is it legal?"

I rolled mine. "Of course it is! Why would you ask something like that?"

He shrugged. "Because in movies, when someone says that, it's usually not."

"Well, this is legal. Not only is it legal, but it's official," I replied. "Meaning I'm even going to *pay* you for your time."

His eyes lit up. "With money?"

"No. Even better. With fried Oreos."

He shook his head. "I'm off the Oreos," he said. "I've moved on to Coca-Cola cake. You ever had it?"

I shook my own.

"Well, it's awesome. It's an international thing."

"It is?"

"Well, not exactly international," he admitted. "More like . . . southern."

Because people who had only lived in Manhattan tended to think it was the center of the universe, anywhere outside of the city pretty much was considered a foreign country to them.

"Can you get it at street fairs?" I asked. That's where I had had to get the fried Oreos last time. Lucky for me, the campaign had taken place during the height of the street fair season so it hadn't been too much of a problem.

"Nope. But you can get it at that new bakery on sixty-eighth and Amsterdam," he replied. "They also have these things called pralines that are from New Orleans. They're *awesome*. So what's the business proposition?"

"So my mom is finally marrying Laurel's dad and I get to give the toast at the wedding, and I thought it would be cool to make a video toast," I said. "And because you did a good job on the video campaign, I thought I'd ask you if you'd help me."

He nodded. "I did do a great job on that one, didn't I?" he asked. "Maybe I should drop out of school and just start making films. I bet I could get an agent and everything."

I rolled my eyes. "It was pretty good."

"Pretty good?! It got you *elected*!"

"It was *one* of the things that got me elected," I shot back. "The fact that I have a non-threatening personality and I smell like watermelon helped, too." I wasn't exactly sure what a "non-threatening personality" was, but at one point during the campaign while I was in the stall of the bathroom near the cafeteria I had overheard Odile Majer tell Claudia Lowenstein that. And Alice had reported back on the watermelon comment, made by Kurt Ogilvy when I sent her to overlisten (because it was overlistening and not eavesdropping, it wasn't like it was illegal or anything). Kurt was known for having an oversensitive nose and liked to compare everything to smells.

He leaned forward and sniffed. "I don't smell anything watermelon-like."

"So do you want to help me or not?" I asked, moving back. It wasn't so much that I was worried that he could smell me as much as the fact that I had a slight suspicion that I was getting my period at that very instant. Stress and excitement were known to bring it on (at least according to Marissa), and I had definitely had a lot of both of those lately.

He shrugged. "Okay."

"Great," I said.

"But I'm not sure I want to be paid in Coca-Cola cake," he said. "I might want it in some other sort of dessert currency."

I looked at my watch. It was already eight-thirty and I hadn't even watched the episode of *Come On, People—Get with the Program* that I had DVRed earlier. If it turned out that I did get my period, that was going to push me back even further. "Can we decide on the payment stuff at another time?"

"I guess so," he replied. "I'll start writing a contract up and e-mail it to you."

Yeah, well, we'd see about that. So far his track record with following up on his promises to get in touch was about as good as my promise to Mom to keep my room clean for longer than three hours.

chapter 5

Dear Dr. Maude,

Not to tell you how to run your business or anything, but if you had a Yelp page where people could leave comments and ratings, I'm pretty sure you'd only average like one star and some very not-so-good comments about the fact that you don't return people's e-mails. And because a lot of people base their decisions on those comments—like, say, Sarah, my dad's girlfriend-slash-mother-of-Ziggy-my-half-brother—this might eventually make you lose a lot of your popularity. Which would mean no one would watch your TV show anymore or buy your books. And ultimately you'd end up with no money and you'd have to get a job as a waitress at a diner or something like that.

Or who knows—maybe it's just MY letters that you're not returning. Which therefore makes you guilty of discrimination, a subject I feel very passionate about. (If you remember from when I ran for class president, my whole campaign platform was that I was going to try my best to stop dork discrimination.) (Which, BTW, I've been very successful at.) (But seeing that you NEVER READ MY LETTERS you probably didn't know that.)

But the reason I'm writing today is not to tell you how disappointed I am about the fact that you never write me back (even though I am). It's to ask for some advice. Okay, so you know how our family is being taped for Wendi Wallerstein's show? (You'd know that if you read my e-mails.) Well, Laurel and I sort of got into a fight on-camera. Not really a fight, because Laurel would never do that on national television since her publicist would yell at her and tell her it would ruin her image. But she totally embarrassed me by basically telling all of America that I'm on the messy side. WHICH IS NOT TRUE—I'm just CREATIVELY ORGANIZED. If you ever want to come over, I'll show you my room so you can see that I'm not lying.

Even though we're not exactly in a fight-fight, Laurel and I are not really talking. If I went to my mother and told her what was going on, she'd probably say, "Lucy, sometimes it's better to just put your ego aside and go and be the bigger person and start talking to her as if everything is fine." But (a) I can't even go to my mother because SHE'S acting all weird, too, and (b) I'm a little sick of being the bigger person all the time.

Is there any way to fix this situation that does not include me doing anything bigger-person-like?

yours truly,
LUCY B. PARKER

"Oh! Oh! I know!" Alice gasped the next day at lunch, waving her arm around as if we were sitting in a classroom rather than at a cafeteria table.

"Yes, Alice?" I asked.

"You could e-mail yourself for advice about what to do about Laurel," she replied.

I shook my head. "No. This one is too hard," I said glumly. "I don't think even I can come up with the answer to this." I had tried, for hours last night. I had even tried to enlist Miss Piggy's help by locking her in the room with me, snuggling her, and whispering the whole thing into her ear. (I didn't want to risk Laurel hearing in case she was standing at the door overlistening or something.) But all I got were some scratches on my arms.

Before Alice could wave her hand with another idea, Malia tapped me on the shoulder. "Cristina Pollock at nine o'clock," she said.

We all turned to see a girl who looked like she had just sucked on a lemon striding over to our table. The fact that she had left Kansas to come over to Arizona was NOT a good sign. Usually when Cristina did that it was to threaten me about something—like when she told me that if I ran for class president against her I'd be seriously sorry. (Which, BTW, I ended up not being on account of the fact that I *beat* her.)

As usual, her long blonde hair flowed and bounced behind her like the actresses in shampoo commercial. It really wasn't fair that someone so mean had such good hair. I wondered if it was a karma thing. Although the idea that Cristina had been nicer in a past life was hard to imagine.

"Hello, *Lucy*," she said as she flipped her hair.

Unlike Beatrice, who had no problem rolling her eyes in front of Cristina, I was only brave enough to do it in my mind. Maybe if I had once been BFFs with Cristina before being dumped like Beatrice had it wouldn't have been so hard, but because Cristina was known as not only the most popular girl at the Center but also the meanest, I didn't feel like taking any chances.

"Hi, Cristina!" I said, all friendly. "How are you today? That blue sweater goes really well with your eyes." I left out the fact that I knew it was from Laurel's new clothing line that had just started selling at Always 16. Cristina totally tried to copy Laurel all the way from her head (long, layered haircut) to her feet (the same lilac Uggs that Laurel had worn in the latest episode of her show, also for sale at Always 16 but in knockoff style); it was pretty lame. Instead I was practicing what Dr. Maude called "reverse psychology," which was where, in hopes of getting someone to do what you want, you did the OPPOSITE of what you really felt like saying or doing. Like, say, being really nice to someone who was always really mean to you.

She wrinkled her nose as if I had just said, "Hi, Cristina! You know, sometimes when I eat too many pickles, my stomach gets all wonky and I end up burping a lot." "Yeah, well, *anyway*," she said, all snotty. "So I was wondering what a person has to do to get an invitation to that wedding."

"What wedding?" I asked innocently.

She rolled her eyes. "Um, your mother and Laurel's father's?" she said as if I were super dumb. "It's all over those *Week with Wendi* commercials."

Right. The commercials. Mom had *not* been happy when she heard about those. Even though the show was nowhere near to being on TV yet, because Laurel was such a big star, from the minute she had agreed to do the show, the network had started advertising it. When you're trying to keep a wedding quiet, having it announced on national television every commercial break didn't help. Suddenly, Mom's phone was ringing off the hook with calls from people she hadn't talked to in years.

"And on Austin's Twitter feed. He just Tweeted that Laurel invited him," she added.

My eyes widened. What?! Okay, yes, so Laurel and I weren't getting along so great at the moment but the fact that Austin was coming was BIG news. How could Laurel—as my BFF *and* frister—not tell me about this first? Was this part of The Change? Like, because she was older and famous she now got to do whatever she wanted? And what about the whole this-wedding-is-only-going-to-be-immediate-family thing? My *grandmother* wasn't even invited—and because she followed Austin on Twitter, she was now going to know he was coming *and* be really mad about that.

I rummaged in my I Hate Mean People Even Though It's Mean to Hate tote bag for my phone. (When you had to lug around various logs and a notebook called "Important Pieces of Advice," a regular old purse wasn't big enough. Which was why I now had almost as many tote bags as I did pairs of Chuck Taylor sneakers.) Right before I pushed Laurel's name in the address book, I remembered that they were shooting a scene from her sitcom at Billy's Bakery that afternoon. Forget about trying to handle this on the phone—I needed to handle this in person.

And not just because Billy's was my most favorite place in New York City.

Since they had the most delicious cupcakes in the world, Billy's was always crowded to begin with, but with the crew there from Laurel's show it was even *more* crowded—not to mention very hot because of all the bright lights. I had learned from the time I went to L.A. with Laurel that movie sets were definitely not the greatest place for people with coordination issues to hang out because of the fact that there were lots of expensive things to bump into and break. Which is why I stayed near the back with my friends until I felt like it was a good time to confront Laurel about inviting Austin without getting permission was totally unfair. Plus, that's where the craft services table was, which had unlimited snacks ... for free (including cupcakes, my favorite food).

A red-headed, freckled-faced woman with braids wearing overalls and a walkie-talkie strapped to her right hip ran up to us and plucked the red velvet cupcake I was just about to take a giant bite of out of my hand. This was Cricket, the Second AD, which stood for assistant director. I had heard from Laurel—back when we were getting along—that Cricket was a little on the bossy side. ("Honey, that's not very nice," Alan had said when Laurel had brought it up during one of our official family dinners. "'Overenthusiastic' is a much nicer term.")

"Hey! What are you doing?" I cried.

"Didn't you hear me yell all extras on set! ASAP?" she barked.

"But we're not extras," I replied, standing on my tiptoes for the cupcake but missing, because although my boobs had missed the no-more-growing memo, the rest of me had not.

"Then what are you girls doing here?" she demanded.

"Hey, has anyone ever told you look a lot like Pippi Longstocking?" Alice asked excitedly.

I looked at Alice and gave a little shake of my head. According to Laurel, Cricket was *very* sensitive about that.

As usual, Alice just kept right on going. "Your braids even stand up at the ends like hers do!" She leaned in for a closer look. "How does that happen? Do you put wire in there or something?"

I stepped in front of her. "I'm Lucy B. Parker. Laurel's frister?"

Alice ducked her head around. "That's a combination of friend and sister," she explained. "Isn't that neat? Once the wedding happens, then they'll be stepsisters, but Lucy doesn't like that word, so she came up with 'frister' and—"

I put my hand over Alice's mouth to shut her up.

Cricket's eyes narrowed. "How do I know that's true? How do I know you're not some crazed fan who's going to reach into your pocket and take out a pair of scissors and snip a lock of her hair to then use in some spell you found in a book at a Wiccan bookstore? Because that happened to Miley once. Or *would've*, had I not stepped in."

"Um, because I don't lie since it's bad for your karma?"

Cricket took out her walkie-talkie. "Red Earth to Swan Song—possible stalker situation here," she growled. "Copy."

"I'm not a stalker!" I cried.

"She's not," Malia chimed in. "She doesn't even stalk Blair Lerner-Moskovitz, her unofficial official local crush."

I cringed. I loved my friends but they definitely tended to forget that less was more when it came to talking about my personal life to total strangers.

Beatrice shook her head. "I know I said I was okay with you crushing on my brother, and I'm not going to go back on that, but I just have one question: Why, out of all the boys in Manhattan, *him*?"

This was not the time to be having this conversation. "Look, if you could just get Laurel over here, I can explain." Lucky for me, just then Laurel walked out dressed in a bubblegum pink velour tracksuit—a very Madison-like look. "Laurel!" I yelled. Unluckily for me, she didn't answer, which didn't help my case with Cricket. "Laurel!" I yelled, louder. This time, she looked over but didn't acknowledge me. Then I remembered—she liked to stay in character on set. "Madison," I called out.

At that, she came bounding over. "Hola, chicas!" she bubbled, giving us all hugs. This staying in character thing was getting really annoying. "Hola, chica!" was the way Madison greeted everyone, which, for some reason, always got her a huge laugh from the studio audience on Friday nights when she taped the show. And if for some reason it didn't, then they just added it with the fake-laugh machine.

"You know these people?" Cricket asked suspiciously.

Laurel/Madison nodded. "Yeah. It's okay. In fact, it's . . . *fantabulous* that they're here!" She turned to me. "What do you think? Catchy, right? I'm thinking of trying that out in the next scene."

"It's great," I said. "I can already see the T-shirt. Listen, I need to ask you something."

I turned my back toward Cricket, but she just moved closer. Sheesh. This wasn't overlistening—this was plain old eavesdropping, which was *very* rude.

"It's okay, Cricket," Laurel said,

"You're sure?" she asked again, just as doubtfully. "Because in addition to being a second AD, I also happen to be a self-defense instructor."

"Thanks, but it's fine," Laurel said. "You can go."

After Cricket walked away, I turned to her. "How could you invite Austin to the wedding?"

She looked confused. "What are you talking about? I didn't," she replied. "That would be breaking rule number one on the Official Rules of the Parker-Moses Family Wedding list that says, 'Wedding will be restricted to immediate family.'" The way she said it, kind of in her dust-is-a-silent-killer tone, was definitely not Madison-esque.

"Yeah, well, apparently he doesn't know that because he Tweeted that you did."

"What?!" she cried.

"Did you say anything that would've made him *think* that he was coming?" I asked.

"No. All I said was 'Boy, it would be so great if you could be at the wedding.'" Suddenly she looked nervous. "But when I said it, he was on location in the mountains in Colorado 'cause he's shooting *Monkeyin' Around 5* and the cell reception was really spotty, so maybe what he *thought* I said was 'You should come to the wedding.'" she added. "How am I going to tell them he's coming?!"

"You don't have to," I said. "Because he's not."

"What do you mean?"

"You didn't actually *invite* him," I explained.

"Well, no, but because he thinks I did, I can't now *un*invite him!" I could tell that she was trying to look concerned. From the way she was moving her weight from one foot to the other, either she was really excited or she had to go to the bathroom really bad. She let out a little squeal. "Omigod—if Vermont is half as pretty as it looks in the pictures, this is going to be so romantic!"

"I can't believe I finally have something interesting to tweet!' Alice exclaimed as she whipped out her iTouch.

I grabbed it from her. "No, you don't. 'Cause he's not coming!" From the second that I had found out my mom was dating Alan this had been my biggest fear—Laurel would get whatever she wanted, whenever she wanted, because of who she was. And now it was happening.

"Lucy, I really feel like you're overreacting," Laurel said in her best I-may-not-be-all-that-much-older-than-you-but-I'm-still-older voice. "I mean, sure, this isn't the best way for this to have happened. But because Austin is my boyfriend, he's almost like family."

"Well then if Austin is coming"—I grabbed Beatrice's

arm—"then Beatrice is, too. Because as my BFF, she's almost like family, too. You're not the only one who gets to go inviting people without asking."

"I didn't *ask* him," she said. "He mis*heard* it."

"Oh, like that's any better?" I said. What was going on here? Laurel and I barely ever fought and now, it was all we were doing.

"Fine. Do what you want," Laurel sniffed. "Now if you'll excuse me, I have a show to shoot."

"That's fine," I sniffed back, "because I"—what did I have to do?—"have a cupcake to eat," I said, grabbing a banana one.

I came home later to find Mom sitting at the kitchen table looking like a character on one of those crime shows being questioned by a detective. If detectives dressed all in pink and chirped.

Wendi turned to the camera and leaned in. "*Marriage*," she said dramatically. "The *biggest* and *most important* commitment a person can ever make to another human being."

Mom turned a little yellow as she gave a nervous laugh. "You make it sound so...*serious*," she said.

"That's because it *is!*" Wendi chirped.

"Well, yes, but it's also...Can we change the subject and talk about something else?" she pleaded.

Wendi stood up and began to slowly walk around

the table. "Now, I'm no psychologist, but you know what *I* think, Rebecca?" she asked, as her heels clicked.

"What?" Mom said nervously.

"*I* think that you're a little . . . *nervous* about this upcoming wedding," she said as she clacked.

"Nervous?" Mom peeped. "Why would I be nervous?! Especially because, as I keep telling anyone who will listen, even though no one *is* listening, it's not a wedding, it's a—" Just then she saw me. "Oh, look! There's Lucy. Lucy, why don't you come join us and tell us about your day?"

As Nikko turned around, he caught me on tape shoving half a cupcake in my mouth. (I had taken a few for the road.) Before I could respond—although I wasn't sure "Mmmffff" was much of an answer—Alan came rushing into the room dragging Laurel by the hand. "Oh good—you're both here! I'm calling a family meeting STAT."

"*Fantastic!*" Wendi trilled. "I'm so glad we're here for it. Nikko, make sure you get every second of this," she ordered. She turned to us. "Don't mind us. Just pretend we're not here, okay?"

Mom gave her a doubtful look.

"We're just . . . flies on the wall. Not making a peep."

"We don't have flies," I said, mouth safely free of cupcake. (Except, I would see, later on when it aired, not cupcake *frosting*—there was a big blob on the left corner of my mouth.)

"That's right, Lucy," Alan said. "And do you know *why* we don't have flies?"

"Because we're not allowed to eat outside of the kitchen." I sighed. Back in Northampton I had been able to eat wherever I wanted. Sure, once in a while I came across a fly, or an ant, but I didn't mind. I was going to have to ask Marissa if kids had any say in what happened during this whole Change thing, because if so, I was going to change it so that I could eat in my bedroom without sneaking around.

"Okay, then. I'll just . . . act normal, then," Mom said. She cleared her throat. "Alan, honey, you need to calm down."

That sounded about as real as the one time I tried out for a role in our school play in fifth grade and was told very nicely by Mr. Richards, the gym-slash-drama teacher that I'd probably do better with something in, say, the chorus. Except Ms. Edut, my chorus teacher, had asked me to mouth the words because my singing voice was so bad.

Wendi turned to Nikko. "Are you getting this?" she asked in a loud whisper.

As he nodded, the camera bobbed up and down and hit Siouxie the makeup woman in the shoulder.

"Ow!" she yelled.

"Flies on the wall, people," Wendi hissed. "Flies on the wall."

"Who says I'm not calm?!" Alan cried. Unlike

Mom, he was having no trouble being himself. His very nervous self. "I'm calm. Well, as calm as a person can be about the fact that our very small wedding in a very small town is now going to be overrun by people with cameras!"

Even though I was not a fan of the I-told-you-so look, I couldn't stop myself from giving Laurel one. I *knew* I was right in thinking that Laurel's screwup was going to be a big deal.

"I don't mean to interrupt," Wendi interrupted, "but as you can see, because it's very important to me to create a real sense of intimacy with my subject, I make sure to only have one camera in the room—"

Mom went from yellow to green. "What do you mean it's going to be overrun by people with cameras?"

Alan turned to Laurel, who now looked a lot less sure of herself than she had back on set. "Laurel, tell Rebecca what happened," he said somewhat sternly.

"Yeah, Laurel. Tell her what happened," I added.

After giving me a look, she screwed her eyes shut. "Austin kind of sort of now thinks he's invited to the wedding!"

I waited for Mom to go completely ballistic, but nothing happened. Not even a twitch of her eyebrow, which always happened when I brought up Operation New Kitten.

Wendi gasped. "Austin Mackenzie?!"

Laurel nodded. "It's not like I invited him," she went

on. "It was this misunderstanding because he was on top of a mountain and—"

Wendi clapped. "Ooh—this is *juicy*. In fact, this might make this the highest-rated *Week with Wendi* ever!" She turned to Camilla. "We're holding this for sweeps." I knew from Laurel that sweeps was considered the most important time of the television season. It was when all the Very Special episodes and the ones with the big guest stars were on. Wendi turned to Laurel. "Honey, you don't know who his agent and publicist are, do you? Because I'm thinking I should get in touch with them and see if I can tape him, too."

Laurel's right eyebrow shot up. "I thought this was MY *Week with Wendi.*"

She smiled. "Oh, sweetie, it is! It is!" She turned to Charles and gave a snap. "Find out who the agent is," she whispered.

I leaned in to Mom and squinted to see if I could see anything that showed how mad she was that Laurel would do this without asking. A frown. A sigh. Even just a blink. But there was nothing.

Laurel sighed. "You know what? This is just going to end up getting messy." She walked over and picked up her iPhone. "I'm going to call Austin and tell him that he can't come—"

Mom shook her head and sighed. "No, you're not. It's fine. He can come."

Wait—what?!

"But it's your guys' wedding," Laurel said. "I don't want it to become all about Austin and me."

"Yeah," I agreed. Whoops. Had I said that out loud? I hadn't meant to.

"It's *all* of our wedding," Mom corrected.

"Well, if she gets to invite Austin, then I get to bring Beatrice," I said.

"Lucy, we'll talk about that later," Mom said firmly. She shot a look at Wendi. *"In private."*

"But it's only fair!" I cried.

"Lucy," she said sharply as her right eyebrow shot up.

"Oh, thank you, thank you!" Laurel cried as she threw her arms around her. "You're the best mother in the entire world!"

Wendi pushed Nikko forward. "You better be getting this," she ordered.

"I *am*!" he said.

There were so many things wrong with this situation I didn't even know where to start. First there was Marissa being right about this Change business. Who knew how long I was now going to have to listen to "I hate to say I told you . . . but *I told you so.*" Then there was the fact that Mom had just totally given in to Laurel and was shushing me.

But that wasn't the worst of it—it was Laurel using the word *mother* that had really freaked me out. Sure, I felt beyond awful for Laurel that her mom had died when she was six. I honestly couldn't imagine anything worse happening to a person. Even when Mom was completely embarrassing me by talking about how big my boobs were getting in a voice so loud that people in India could hear her, just thinking about the idea of her not being on this planet to do things like that made my stomach get all rumbly like the way it did right before I was going to start crying. And even though Laurel and I had made fun of all the self-help books that Mom and Alan had bought about how to mix and stir your way into a happy blended family, I had to admit it had worked. We *were* a family, and I loved Laurel like a sister and Alan like a dad.

But even though I was probably doing serious damage to my karma for even just thinking it, I guess I hadn't thought that Laurel would actually think of my mom as *her* mom, too. As a frother (that was friend + mother, which was the term we had come up instead of stepmother), sure, but as a mother? As excited as I was about the wedding the idea of really, *really* sharing my mom—like in an official way—suddenly felt a bit scary. What if, as part of The Change, she started loving Laurel more than me?

Alan walked over and got in on the hug. "I'm really proud of how you two handled that," he said. "That was excellent conflict resolution!"

As I stood off to the side, I couldn't deny that The Change was happening. To the point where I was now totally left out.

chapter 6

Dear Dr. Maude,

I've been thinking a lot about this and I'm worried that the reason you're not writing back to me is because you think that I have a bit of a girl-who-cried-wolf thing going on. Looking back at my e-mail file where I keep all of the e-mails I sent you (I may not be organized in other areas of my life, but I'll have you know that when it comes to my friendship with you, I'm VERY organized), I noticed that more than a few times I mentioned that whatever it was I needed advice on was VERY, VERY important—like, more important than anything else I had written to you before—and therefore I really, really, REALLY needed you to write back to me right away.

Well, as much as you probably don't believe me at the moment, this time I'm not kidding when I say that this time it IS very important that you get back to me. We're talking more important than ever.

And the reason for that is that things with Laurel and me are bad. Like, really, really, REALLY bad. Probably worse than they've ever been. I don't have the time to go back and see if I've ever written that exact sentence to you in the past, but trust me when I tell you it's true.

And it's not just Laurel—it's this whole Change thing, and the way that Mom didn't even get the tiniest bit mad when she found out that Austin thought that Laurel was inviting him even though he just heard her wrong because he was on top of a mountain. And then how when I said, "Well, if Austin gets to be there, then I'm bringing Beatrice," she said, "Lucy, we'll talk about it later." And then it took TWENTY-SEVEN HOURS for me to pin her down to do that. (She did say yes, which is good.)

I thought that officially becoming a family was going to make things better, but, frankly, if things are going to continue to go like this, then I don't think it is. In fact, they might even get WORSE.

Not only that, but as hard as I try, I can't seem to get into the mood to work on my video toast for the wedding—the thing that was going to prove that Laurel isn't the only talented person in the family. It's like I have toast block or something. So if you have advice for that, too, that would be great.

Thanks in advance.

yours truly,
LUCY B. PARKER

"Did you get knocked on the head and get amnesia or something?" Blair asked later as he slumped on our living room couch crunching on some chocolate-covered pretzels I had smuggled out of the kitchen. "I mean how hard can it be to come up with a few examples of fun times you've had with your sister? Even I can come up with some and I can't stand mine."

It used to be that I couldn't *not* think of fun times I had had with Laurel because there were so many of them. But for the last hour my mind was totally blank. I stopped pacing and turned to him. "I'm just . . . it's just . . ." I sputtered before plopping down in a chair. "You wouldn't understand." My brain was so exhausted from all the wracking I had been doing that when I saw Blair drop half a pretzel in between the cushions I didn't even say anything. I figured if things kept going the way they were and Laurel kept being everyone's favorite, I could just move back to Northampton and no one would really care. And by the time the pretzel was discovered between the cushions I'd be long gone.

"Try me," Blair said.

"It's just that ever since my mom and Laurel's dad chose a wedding date, everything's different."

"Ohhh. You mean The *Change*." He nodded. "Yeah, that stuff is *rough*."

How was it that everyone in the world except me knew about this Change business?

He reached for more pretzels and promptly dropped a few on the rug without even noticing. "My friend Sam?" he said with his mouth full. "Things got so bad between him and his stepsister that his parents tried to convince him he was crazy and sent him away to a *mental hospital.*"

"Really?" I gasped.

He shrugged. "No, but it sounds good."

I threw a pretzel at him. "Well, I read a script once for Laurel where the character got sent to a mental hospital against her will and it was awful," I said. "Her parents told her that they had a surprise for her and then—bam—they threw her in there. Although because it's a hospital she got to eat dessert before dinner, which was pretty cool."

"Pre-dinner desserts are the best," Blair agreed.

I was glad that I had picked a local crush with whom I was very in sync with on the food front.

Just then my phone beeped with a text from my mom. I paled.

"What's the matter?" Blair asked.

"It's from my mom. *Can you come meet me at the corner of 72nd and Columbus? I have a surprise for you.*"

We looked at each other.

Usually I loved those words. But today? Not so much.

Just to be safe, before I left the house I packed my laptop, two changes of clothes, all my savings ($22.57), a healthy supply of maxi- and minipads, and my passport. I didn't know what Mom's idea of a surprise was, but I wasn't taking any chances in case I found myself having to make a run for it.

"Lucy, I know that the last few weeks have been a little strange," Mom said as we walked up Broadway.

A *little*?! I didn't even want to know what she considered "a lot."

"Obviously, it's a time of transition," she went on.

I glanced behind at my knapsack to make sure nothing had fallen out. Was this transition going to include me having to bolt? I sure hoped not, because if they gave out grades for cardio, I'd get, like, a C minus.

"Even though, if you ask me, people are making a much bigger deal out of this even than they need to," she said. "But that's another subject—"

As we came up on Town Shop Lingerie on our left, I held my breath. Was the surprise new bras? Because if it was, I was so making a break for it.

"At any rate, last night Alan and I were talking and we thought with all the change that's going on, why not throw in more and—"

I exhaled as we passed it and kept walking.

"—let you get a kitten. We're going to Petco."

My mouth dropped open so wide you could have fit the M72 bus in it.

Mom nodded. As she smiled, I realized it was the first non-fake I'm-going-to-kill-the-next-person-who-brings-up-this-wedding smile I had seen in a long time.

"For real?" I asked, dazed. I threw myself toward her and smothered her in a hug. "Thankyouthankyouthank-you!" I cried.

She laughed—a real laugh. "Don't thank me yet. First you have to find her. Or him. You need to choose carefully—it's a big decision."

I took a deep breath and nodded. That was true. This wasn't like choosing which pair of Chuck Taylors out of my collection to wear. This was going to be Miss Piggy's sister or brother. For a second I wondered whether I should ask if we should go home and get Miss Piggy and bring her so she could be part of the decision making, too, but then I remembered how much she hated being out of the house and the weird noises she made. The last time we had brought her to the vet, the cab driver said that she sounded like a sick goat. "I will," I said solemnly as we continued walking.

Once we got to Petco, we made our way to the adoption area. There were so many cats to choose from. There were older tabbies who were so fat they looked like they had pinheads. Silver-colored Siamese cats who meowed nonstop. Fluffy little Persians who looked like ragweeds.

And then I saw her.

People talk about love or crushes at first sight in terms of people, but I totally believe it happens with animals, too. There was nothing particularly special about this one. She was small and scrawny and all black, and she didn't even look that soft, like the mountain of sleeping kittens piled up on top of each other in the corner of the same cage. But the minute I saw her trying to gnaw on the metal bars before sticking her head through the side and getting it stuck, I knew she was mine. If I were a cat, getting my head stuck is totally something I'd do. And when the woman who worked there told me that she had been adopted by someone else the week before but then returned because the person wanted a kitten that was less "rambunctious" (when I looked it up on dictionary.com, I found that it meant hyper-like), I knew even more that the whole thing was fate.

"That's her," I said to Mom.

"Are you sure?" she asked as we watched her try to chase her tail but fail miserably.

"Uh-huh. Look—she's even got coordination issues."

"What do you think her name is?" Mom asked.

I didn't even have to take out my "Miscellaneous" notebook and turn to the list titled "Possible Cat Names Once I Finally Convince Mom and Alan to Let Me Get One." Because the kitten had the same kind of look on her face that Dr. Maude gave her guests when they were on the crazy side—kind of a Oh-my-God-did-you-REALLY-just-say-that-because-you-sound-REALLY-nuts-right-now look, it was completely clear.

"Her name is Dr. Maude," I announced.

"Okay, then," Mom said. "Let's take Dr. Maude home."

I knew there were a lot of books about how to blend families because Alan owned all of them, but I had really wished someone had written one about how to blend pets because I sure could've used one that night.

In the movie in mind, I had always dreamed that when I got a new kitten, not only would it love me best, but as soon as Miss Piggy saw it, all of her meanness would disappear as she fell madly in love with this little kitten that she could teach to do various cat things. (Not that Miss Piggy did anything other than sleep, eat, and throw up hairballs. She didn't even like to play with toys—which I had learned the hard way after, in an attempt to buy her love, I spent almost all my allowance on toys five weeks in a row.) Unfortunately, when we got home, a different movie played out. One that was more like a horror movie.

When we opened the door, Laurel and Alan were waiting in the living room.

"Where is she?" Laurel asked excitedly.

Okay, I'm sorry, but Laurel hadn't even *liked* cats before she met Miss Piggy.

"In here," I said, holding the carrier even closer to my chest. While Mom had reminded me during the cab ride home that Dr. Maude was a *family* pet, I needed time to make it love me the best before Laurel got her hands on it.

"Let me see," she said, running up to it and sticking her face down to the mesh to get a better look. "Ohhhh ...she's so ... OW!" she yelled as Dr. Maude tried to nip her on the nose through the mesh.

"What happened?! Are you okay?! Did it break the skin?!'" Alan cried. He turned to Mom. "It has its rabies shot, right?"

I held Dr. Maude closer to me. "She's not big on strangers," I said. It wasn't like I wanted Dr. Maude to *hurt* Laurel, but I had to admit I was relieved that Dr. Maude hadn't instantly fallen in love with Laurel like Miss Piggy had. I began to walk toward my room.

"Where are you going?" Laurel asked. "All the Google results say that when you bring home a new cat, it's best to put it in a room by itself with the door closed for a while so that the two cats can get used to each other's smell before you actually put them face-to-face."

I shook my head. "It's okay," I said. "Miss Piggy and I have already discussed this. It'll be fine," I said as I went into my room and shut the door.

I found Miss Piggy where she always was: in the corner trying to groom herself but repeatedly falling over because she was so fat. For some reason she seemed to like my room the best . . . as long as I wasn't in it. "Miss Piggy, I have a surprise for you," I said in my sweetest voice. "I think you're really going to like it." I cringed. I sounded so sweet I was giving myself a toothache.

She looked up and gave me a yeah-right look.

"It's in here," I said, patting the carrier. At that, Dr. Maude gave the cutest little meow I had ever heard. It was sweet and dainty and everything that I was not but sometimes wished I could be. Not to mention, she totally understood English.

Miss Piggy struggled to her feet, and her ears went back. Maybe not the most welcoming reaction in the world, but I knew that once I opened the carrier and she got a look at Dr. Maude they'd be instant BFFs.

"Because I have Laurel, I didn't want you to feel left out, so I got you a frister of your own!" That was true. So what if I left out the part about how I thought it would be nice to have a pet who didn't hate me.

"So now, without further ado—meet Dr. Maude!" I cried as I unzipped the carrier.

The next part was a blur. There was a lot of yowling, a lot of fur flying, and what I'm pretty sure was one giant fart from Miss Piggy before Dr. Maude leaped on my head (a good way to discover her nails definitely needed a clipping) before scrambling under the covers.

"Lucy, is everything okay in there?" I heard Mom yell.

"Yup—everything's fine!" I panted as I patted my head feeling for blood.

"I told her she should have followed the advice to introduce them slowly," I heard Laurel say.

"I know you did, honey," I heard Mom reply.

I rolled my eyes. I couldn't even remember the last time I was honey'd or sweetie'd. "I don't need advice!" I called out stubbornly. "I'm an official advice *giver*!"

As I reached for my iTouch so I could Google "what to do when your cat tries to kill another cat," Dr. Maude

113

popped her little head out from under the covers. "See, Miss Piggy? She just wants to be friends."

Miss Piggy cocked her head and thought about it. Then, after what I swear was a nod, she began to make her way toward us. By this time, Dr. Maude had wriggled out from under the covers and climbed up on my shoulder and had begun to nibble on my ear. "I knew you'd come around," I said as I started to relax. "Believe me, no one knows better than me how hard change is, but you'll see. Having a frister—"

Before I could finish with "—is the best thing in the world," Miss Piggy jumped up on the bed and lunged at Dr. Maude, setting off another flying furfest.

After I managed to pry them apart with only a few scratches on my arms, I flopped back on the bed.

Maybe Miss Piggy knew something I didn't.

"Whoa, *chica*—what's goin' on?" Pete asked the next day as I dragged myself into the building after school. "Don't take this the wrong way, but you look like something the cat dragged in."

At the word *cat*, I cringed. "That's because I didn't get much sleep last night."

"Well, babies'll do that to you," he said. "You know that from your time with Ziggy."

Actually, I didn't, because when I was around Ziggy, I turned into a baby whisperer and could make him fall—and stay—asleep immediately. I shook my head. "It's not because Dr. Maude's a baby." I yawned. "It's because I had to stay awake to make sure Miss Piggy didn't eat her." I had tried to set up a kittycam by turning on Skype on my laptop and trying to sync it with FaceTime so I could watch them while I was at school, but I was too tired to get my head to work that way and too embarrassed to ask Blair for his help.

"Well, they'll be getting along soon enough," he said. "These things take time. Remember how it was with you and Laurel at first? And look at you guys now—you're inseparable!"

"Actually, we're not talking," I said glumly as I caught the Gummi Worm he threw my way.

"Still?"

I nodded, trying not to let my face fall into the plant on his desk. "It's one of those things where because we haven't talked for a while, it would be weird at this point to just start again, so we're not," I explained. I shook my head. "It's this wedding. It's making everyone all nuts. Last night I walked into the kitchen and found my mom shoveling ice cream in her mouth with one hand and cookies with the other."

He thought about it for a second. "What's wrong with that?"

It was exactly things like that that explained why Pete was my best adult friend. He may have been a fifty-year-old Puerto Rican guy from Queens, but we were so alike it was scary. "Nothing's wrong with it other than the fact that Mom's idea of a wild and crazy dessert is a Fruit Roll-Up."

"Eh, so she's just a nervous bride," he said. "It happens. Believe me, as a doorman, I know about these things."

"Yeah, well, we're not even allowed to use the words *bride* or *groom*. Or *wedding*." I shook my head. "If they're going to have a wedding, they should just have a wedding, you know? So all the people we love can be there. Like you."

"Aw, Lucy, I thought you'd never ask!" he cried. "I'd be *honored*."

At that, I sat up straight. I was no longer exhausted. Instead, I felt like I had drunk three Red Bulls even though they were number one on the official Parker-Moses No Eating/Drinking list. "Huh?"

He rubbed his hands together. "This is going to be great." He rummaged in the drawer for the schedule. "I just gotta see who I can swap days with for that weekend—"

I was just . . . talking. Off the top of my head. I wasn't inviting him to the wedding. "Wait, what I meant was—" I started to say.

He got up and came over and gave me a hug. After he let me go and he took my cheeks in his hands, the mist in his eyes had turned to full-blown tears. "You know, in my line of work, I come across a lot of different kind of people," he said. "And part of the doorman's code of ethics is 'Thou shall not play favorites.' But in the case of your family, that's impossible. Because the four of you? You're just the best. And I wouldn't miss this wedding for the world." After he kissed me on the forehead, he let go of my cheeks. "Now what were you going to say?"

I could do this. Wasn't Pete always telling me to be direct and just be myself? I could tell him that he had misunderstood me and I hadn't actually invited him to the wedding because to do something like that without first talking to Mom and Alan would not go over well. Especially when Mom was already acting all stressy. Except, of course, if I did it in front of Wendi. Then it might not be so bad. "I was going to say . . ."

"Before you go on, I just wanna say I'm so touched that you would include me, Lucy. It means the world to me." He blew his nose into the handkerchief he carried around in the pocket of his doorman jacket. "Now that's the last thing I'm going to say. The floor is now yours."

I took a deep breath. "I was going to say . . . I should really get upstairs . . . to check on the cats. You know, to make sure they're still alive." So much for coming clean and being direct.

"Okay," Pete said. "That's good because with the wedding coming up, I don't really have the time to be chatting. There's a lot I have to do before now and then."

So did I. Like figure out how to get myself out of this mess.

I walked into the living room to find Mom and Alan sitting on the couch holding hands, explaining to Wendi how they had met, when Alan hired Mom to be Laurel's on-set tutor in Northampton. (Mom was a writer, but because she had been working on the same novel for eight years, the way she made money was tutoring.) Actually, it was more Alan who was explaining it all, on account of the fact that Mom was busy unwrapping miniature Reese's Peanut Butter Cups as fast as she could and popping them into her mouth without missing a beat.

Alan turned to her. "Honey? Maybe you could hold off on eating those until *after* we're done filming."

"Bmmffhhmmmrry," came her reply. Most people probably wouldn't understand what she was saying, but it was very clear to me that it translated to "But I'm hungry" because I said that very thing with my mouth full at least once a day.

Alan looked at the camera and flashed a nervous smile. "She's a little hungry. Pre-wedding jitters." He laughed nervously.

She glared at him. "I mean, pre–small—"

Another glare.

"Okay, I'm just going to get back to the story," he said. Luckily, he left out the part about the Hat Incident. "And now, a year later, we've finally agreed on a place to get married," Alan went on. He laughed. "Although I have to say, at times, that felt harder to do than coming up with a plan for peace in the Middle East."

Mom wiped some (but not all) of the chocolate off her face with her hand and flashed a fake smile. "While we have a lot in common, we sometimes have a little trouble when it comes to choosing places to travel."

A *little* trouble? See "having to ask for Lucy's advice-giving expertise when searching for a place to go for their anniversary" for more information.

Alan held up a bunch of menus. "And what to serve at the wed—"—another look from Mom— "—ing."

Mom's popped another Reese's in her mouth. "*Sweetheart*, I'm sure Wendi is sick of hearing about this thing," she said. She gave a little laugh. "I know I am."

"No, no, no! I'd *love* to hear about it!" Wendy squealed. "Viewers just *love* drama!"

This time Mom popped three Reese's in at once. "I don't know what you're talking about," she laughed nervously. "There's no drama. We're a drama-free household."

Alan turned to her. "I have an idea—let's ask Wendi what she thinks about the meal thing. She looks like she has a lot of experience going to weddings."

I shook my head. If that kind of thing came out of the mouth of a Mean Person—like, say, Cristina Pollock, it would be completely obvious that they were just stirring things up with one of those big electric mixers. But in Alan's case, he really was that clueless and was just trying to help. Unfortunately, from the look on Mom's face, he wasn't. At all.

"Oh, I totally do!" Wendi said. She sighed. "Always a bridesmaid but never a bride, though."

Mom's smile got a little smaller. "I have an idea— let's *not* ask Wendi because it's a private issue that is probably of absolutely no interest to anyone but us!" she said through gritted teeth.

Alan turned to Wendi. "Wendi, at weddings, aren't there usually two choices for the meal? Like, for instance, chicken and fish?"

I don't know who the heck came up with the idea of offering people fish at a wedding. Most people— i.e., me—hated fish. And if they were going to do that, it should at least be something decent like fried clams from Friendly's. With tons of tartar sauce on the side.

She nodded. "Absolutely. You know, the last wedding I went to they had this roasted chicken with pomegranate sauce, and it was just *divine*."

Mom's smile twitched. "But, Alan, *darling*, like I keep saying, seeing that there's such a small group, I don't think we need to have two different meal choices."

Nikko put his camera down. "Not to interrupt or anything, but you might want to take into consideration those of us who are vegans."

"Nikko! What are you doing?! Keep shooting!" Wendi cried.

"Okay, okay," he sighed, putting the camera back up on his shoulder.

"That's right," Alan said "How can we forget the vegans! Like Sarah!"

Mom got up and started to pace.

"Honey, you're pacing," he said nervously. "You never pace. Why are you pacing?"

This was true. Unlike Alan, who paced a lot, Mom only did it when she was extra nervous or upset.

"Why does this wedding have to be so ... *weddingly*?!" she cried. "Why can't it just be a nice small gathering with *almost*-immediate family?" she went on.

"Because it *is* a wedding!" Alan cried. "A ceremony where we honor our commitment to each other as life-long partners!"

At the word *commitment*, Mom's face went from green to yellow, like mine had the time I had eaten some cottage cheese that was two weeks past its expiration date.

"And I don't know why you have such a big problem with the word," he went on. "Honestly, Rebecca, the way you've been acting lately, you'd think you were getting ready to have a root canal."

Wendi turned to Nikko. "You're getting this, right?" she whispered. "Please tell me you're getting this. Research shows that there's a huge spike in ratings with on-air fights."

Mom stopped pacing. "We're not fighting!" she said nervously. "We're just having a discussion. In a very passionate manner!" Mom was not a fan of the f-word, but I don't know why she was so against fighting. I had learned from my fights with Laurel that they actually ended up bringing you closer because you got to air out all the stuff that was bothering you so it didn't get stuck inside you like old gum on the bottom of a chair. Suddenly, she saw me. "Look—it's Lucy!" she cried. "Let's talk about Lucy's life for a while now! What's new in your life?"

As Nikko aimed the camera on me, I could feel my face get all red. I cleared my throat and prayed that my forehead wasn't too shiny because that would look very gross to people across the country. "Umm . . ." Sometimes I had a lot of success asking Mom for things in front of other people because it made it harder for her to say no, but I was thinking this was not the time to bring up the fact that Pete now thought he was invited to this wedding that she didn't seem all that interested in going to herself even though she was the bride.

"Before we go on, let me ask you something," Alan interrupted. "If you were at a wedding, wouldn't it make you happy if you found out that you had your choice of what you wanted to eat for the main course—"

"Alan!" Mom cried.

"Okay, okay. I'm sorry to have interrupted you, Lucy. That was very rude of me. So what's going on?"

Mom reached into her bag and pulled out a York Peppermint Pattie. Okay, this was *serious*. "Oh, you know, not much," I said as I inched my way back toward my room. "Nothing that can't wait until later."

Or, you know, *never*.

Between me in my room trying to make sure Miss Piggy didn't devour Dr. Maude (after so many years of not being able to make Miss Piggy stay put in my room, I now found myself unable to make her budge as she gave Dr. Maude a there's-only-room-for-one-of-us-and-I-am-NOT-leaving glare); Laurel in hers practicing her weeping over her discovery that she was blind; Alan surfing the Internet for articles about what to do when your wife-to-be is less than excited about your upcoming wedding; and Mom scarfing down more mini-size candy bars than even *I* would've been able to stomach, there wasn't a lot of QFT (Quality Family Time) going on.

In fact, it seemed like the only time we were together nowadays was when we were being filmed (why Wendi thought her audience would be interested in us bringing our recycling down to the basement didn't make sense to me, but I kept my mouth shut). But even then, we barely talked. Although Wendi started every segment with a whole thing about how we weren't nearly as dysfunctional as the families of the other *Week with Wendi*'s subjects she had followed, we sure didn't come off as all that loving and happy.

"Okay, I'm calling an emergency family meeting," Wendi announced one evening as we played what was probably the most quiet game of Monopoly in history. Well, quiet except for Miss Piggy's low growls and the continual *thump* of Dr. Maude falling onto the floor whenever she tried to jump up on something because unlike most cats—but like me—she had serious coordination problems. While Laurel and I still weren't officially fighting, we sure weren't officially friends. We were barely even talking to each other. And when we did, we were polite, but it was the kind of politeness you'd show to someone you ran into in a girls' room and you were the only ones there.

That being said, I decided to take some of Dr. Maude's (Dr. Maude–Dr. Maude—not the cat–Dr. Maude's) advice about how to make up with people even if you were NOT the one who started the whole thing. I had found it during my most recent search through my DVR library of her shows. According to her, the best thing to do was extend an olive branch. Not, like, an *actual* olive branch with olives on it, as she impatiently told this woman in the audience who had raised her hand to ask whether you had to go to a nursery for one or if she'd be able to find one at Walmart because now that there was a Super Walmart in her town she could get everything from tires to milk to laundry baskets in one place. It was more a fancy way of saying to suck it up and be the bigger person EVEN IF THE OTHER PERSON HAD JUST AS MUCH OF A PART IN THE WHOLE THING.

I leaned in toward Laurel, whose fake blindness miraculously hadn't gotten in the way of her getting ahead of me in the game with four more hotels. "I didn't think non-family members could call family meetings," I whispered. That seemed like a decent-size olive branch to put forward.

I waited for her to say something but she didn't.

"I guess you're not just blind, but *deaf*, too," I said.

Just as she turned to me, Wendi clapped her hands. "Nikko, camera off for a minute."

At that, we all looked at one another. Wendi *never* wanted the camera off. This was serious.

"Look, per my editor, there's been a severe drop in fun over the last few days of footage," she said. "And while research has proven that viewers like drama and conflict and intrigue, they also like *fun*. So to that end, Camilla and I had a call with the network this morning and we've come up with what we all feel is a fabulous way to infuse more fun into things."

"It's not bra shopping, is it?" I blurted out. Because if it was, I was taking Dr. Maude and bolting.

She shook her head. "No. Although that *is* a cute idea." She snapped her fingers. "Charles, write that down." She smiled. "We're going to go ... wedding dress shopping!"

From the look on Mom's face, *she* was ready to bolt.

In the movies wedding dress shopping looks fun, but in real life? Not so much. We were at Saks Fifth Avenue, our third store of the afternoon that Saturday when it got very *unfun*.

Mom held up a flowy multicolored thing. "How about this one?"

I wrinkled my nose as I slumped down in a chair. I was all for color, but this was just wrong. "Maybe if you were getting married on a beach in Hawaii," I said.

At that, Wendi and her crew burst into laughter.

"Lucy, you are just *so* funny!" she chirped.

"Really? You think so?" I asked, sitting up a little straighter. I glanced over at Laurel to see her reaction, but she was too busy rehearsing the scene where she's gotten her sight back and is seeing herself in the mirror for the first time to notice.

Wendi turned to Nikko. "You got that on tape, right? That's going to be a nice bit of comic relief among all this drama of the upcoming wedding."

"I keep telling you—there's no drama!" Mom laughed nervously as she dug in her purse for a mini Mounds bar. It was a good thing Mom had no interest in being an actress because she was *awful* at it.

Nikko rolled his eyes. "Of course I" —as he looked at the camera, his face paled— "didn't. Whoops. Seems I forgot to turn it on."

Wendi snapped her fingers at Charles. "Charles! Put 'Find new cameraman' on my to-do list," she said as she glared at Nikko. When she looked at me, she smiled. "Lucy, love, do you think you can do that again?"

"Do what again?" I asked, confused.

"Say that line about the beach in Hawaii," she replied.

Before I could say, "Um, I hate to tell you this, but this is a REALITY special not a MOVIE where you get to do scenes over and over again," she waved her hand. "Never mind, it's fine. Let's move on. Go back to bonding."

Mom, Laurel, and I just looked at one another.

"Bond! Bond!" Wendi chirped.

We shrugged and continued looking through the racks.

Suddenly, Wendi *click-clacked* over and picked up a frilly, lacy-white-gauzy thing and held it up to Mom. "Oh, this would look just *so* darling on you!"

Mom wrinkled her nose and gently pushed it away. "Thanks, but that's not really my style."

Wendi yanked another white dress off the rack, this one equally girly and nightgowny-looking. "Then how about this one?"

Mom shook her head.

Wendi sighed. "I don't know why so many women don't like to wear white to their second weddings."

"I didn't even wear white to my *first* wedding," Mom said. Because my parents were creative hippy types, their first wedding was held at one of their friend's houses on a farm in upstate New York. I was glad I hadn't been born yet and didn't have to suffer through it. They used to make me watch the DVD of it back when they were still married, and it looked like it had been a super-weird day. There were people playing all sorts of corny instruments like the

127

ukulele and the zither, and instead of a priest or a rabbi doing the whole thing, they had a bunch of friends read different poems, and sing songs. It was like a really bad school talent show but with adults. And Mom wore this funky boho-like patchwork-dress thing that she had gotten in Russia because back when she was single she used to travel all around the world. She still had the dress. She didn't wear it anymore, but she kept it in a fancy plastic cover so it wouldn't get eaten by moths, which was something that had tended to happen in our house in Northampton because it was so old (needless to say, moths—like ants—were not a problem in our New York apartment).

Laurel picked up a yellow dress with a lace collar that was about ten sizes bigger than Mom. "Ooh—this would be perfect for Rose!"

I wrinkled my nose. "That's a little fancy to wear while you cook, don't you think?" I asked.

"No, I meant for the wedding," she replied.

Mom looked over at her. "Laurel, honey, what are you talking about?"

I reached into my Girls Rule . . . Boys Drool tote bag and took out a pen and the small notebook I had started carrying around titled "The Change." *Tuesday, 4:17p.m.— Mom calls Laurel "honey" AGAIN—making that the seventh time this week. # of times she's called ME "honey" this week? ZERO!!!* I wrote. I figured that having all this evidence might come in handy if The Change started to get really out of control.

Laurel cringed. "I . . . kind-of, sort-of ended up . . . *inviting* her to the wedding," she said sheepishly.

"You invited Rose to the wedding?" I asked excitedly. This was great. If Laurel invited Rose, that meant I wouldn't get in trouble for inviting Pete.

Mom glanced over at the camera and put on one of her fake smiles. She was using them more and more and getting a lot better at them. "Laurel, *sweetheart*, we really wanted to keep this a family-only affair, remember?"

 # of "sweethearts"—*5*, I wrote.

"Well, she *is* family," Laurel replied. "She's been with Dad and me since I was five." Oh, so now Rose belonged just to her and Alan? That was definitely something to add to the notebook. "She just looked so sad when I was talking about it."

"Yes, but honey, we said *immediate* family," Mom said.

Another "honey." I should have bought a bigger notebook. At the rate things were going I was going to fill this one by the end of the week.

"She is immediate family—she lives with us five days a week," Laurel replied.

Mom shook her head "Fine," she sighed.

Here was my chance. "Well, if Rose is coming, we should probably invite Pete then, too, don't you think?" I asked innocently.

When Mom turned to me, I could tell from the look on her face that, actually, this was *not* fine. "Lucy, we're not inviting Pete," she said firmly.

"But why?!" I asked.

"Because Pete is not family."

I waited for my "honey" or "sweetheart" but it didn't come. "He is to me!" I cried. "If Austin and Beatrice and Rose are coming, then Pete should be able to!" I glanced at the camera. I really, really hoped this part ended up on the cutting room floor because Pete's feelings would be beyond hurt if saw this.

"Oh, this is *good*," I heard Wendi whisper. "This is *really* good."

So much for that happening.

"Lucy, that's enough," snapped Mom. "I don't want to talk about this anymore right now. We can talk about it later. In private. But the answer is still going to be no."

I had learned my lesson enough times the hard way to know that the longer I waited to come clean about something, the bigger the mess I made. "There's something I should probably tell you, then."

"What?"

"You know how Austin misunderstood Laurel and thought he was invited?"

Mom nodded.

"Well, the same thing happened with Pete," I said.

"You invited Pete to the wedding without asking us?" Mom demanded.

"No! I just told you—he ended up *thinking* he was invited!" I cried. Jeez. If this was a listening-comprehension test, Mom totally would've failed.

Mom put her hands on her hips. Never a good sign. "I have an idea," she said. "Why doesn't everyone just invite everyone they want and we can just broadcast the whole thing on national television?" she cried.

Wendi shook her head. "Don't take this the wrong way, honey," she said, "but I don't think the public would be all that interested." She *click-clacked* over to Laurel and put her hands on her shoulders. "Now if it were *this* one's wedding," she chirped, "that would be TV-worthy. Especially if she were marrying Austin. Talk about a royal wedding!" She looked at her. "Have you guys discussed that possibility, sweetpea?"

Laurel looked at her like she was crazy. "I'm *fourteen*."

Wendi shrugged. "Never too early to start thinking about this stuff."

Mom glared at me. "Lucy Beth Parker, you had no right inviting Pete."

"I just told you I didn't invite him!" I cried.

Wendi poked Nikko. "You're getting this, right?"

Mom shook her head. "And I can't believe I agreed to live my life in a fishbowl like this," she huffed as she started to walk toward the escalator. "I'll meet you girls in the sock department."

At that, Laurel looked like she was going to cry. "But I told you I wouldn't have agreed to do this if you guys didn't want me to," she called after her. She turned to me. "You really should have asked them before you did that, you know."

Huh? What was this about?! Where was the big fristerly pat on the shoulder with an "It's going to be okay—she's just acting super weird nowadays, and as soon as we get home we'll figure out a way to fix things"?

"Wait a minute—so it's okay for *you* to invite Rose, but then when Pete thinks he's invited, even though I didn't actually invite him, *I'm* the one who screwed up?"

"But I told you—Rose is like my family."

"Oh, so now she's *your* family?" I demanded. "Not mine?"

"Lucy, that's not what I meant—"

"Fine. Well, if Rose is your family, then Pete is part of *my* family," I shot back. By saying that I was probably giving up my right to any of Rose's yummy fried plantains, which had become one of my favorite foods since moving to New York, but that meant I'd just have to learn to make them myself.

By this time even more of a crowd had gathered. "But I want Pete to be part of my family, too," she said.

I shook my head. "Nope. You already chose Rose."

Her eyes narrowed. "Okay, now you really *are* being immature."

I narrowed mine. "And now you really *are* embarrassing me in front of not only a camera crew but half of Saks."

Laurel twirled on her heel. "I'm going to the sock department, too."

"Well, I'm . . . not," I huffed. The socks were right

next to the bra department, and with the mood Mom was in, I was not taking any chances. The last thing I needed was to have America watch me be humiliated as some saleswoman talked about how bosomy I was. "I'm staying right here."

"Fine," she huffed as she strode away.

"Fine," I called after her.

After she was gone, I looked over at Wendi and her crew. The way their mouths were in little O's, it was like staring at a bunch of Cheerios. How could I save this? "So, uh, seeing that the camera's still rolling, is there anything you wanted to ask me about?" I asked. "Like, I don't know . . . my advice column I write for the school paper?" I sure hope no one asked me for advice about what to do when your family went nuts because I had no idea. "Okay, then. Well, I guess I'm going to . . . go to the sock department, too," I squeaked as I slithered away.

I don't know why people said weddings were supposed to be such a happy time in your life.

Because this one? Was a mess.

chapter 7

Dear Dr. Maude,

I don't know what the heck is going on, but it's like instead of hot air coming out of the heating vents in our apartment, it's blowing some sort of weird gas that when you inhale, it makes everyone start acting all CRAZY, like what happened in that movie that Austin and Connor did last year. Did you happen to see it? Usually I'm not big on action-adventure movies, but this one was REALLY good, even though it didn't have a monkey in it, like most of their movies do.

The closer we get to the wedding, the less everyone seems to be getting along. Not only do I feel like Mom is being extra nice to Laurel, but now Laurel and I are officially in a fight. That would be bad enough on a regular day, but on a day where we're supposed to be taped spending quality time together by Wendi and her crew it's even worse. I'm sure you know this because you're on TV all the time, but it's HARD having to pretend nothing is wrong when something is.

I kind of feel like I want to call an Emergency Parker-Moses Family Meeting to talk about this stuff, but then I bet Wendi would want to tape it and I do NOT want that to happen. If for some reason I ended up crying or something, I wouldn't want that on national television. I mean, I know you try and get your guests to cry, which is fine and all, but I don't want to be one of those people.

Wish me luck.

yours truly,
Lucy B. Parker

"Now, if you remember," Wendi said as she *clicked* and *clacked* her way across Laurel's not-one-piece-of-clothing-or-dust-bunny-on-it floor. "The last time we saw Laurel and Lucy together, it was not sunny in Philadelphia."

"We don't live in Philadelphia—we live in New York," I said, confused.

She turned to me. "It's a TV series," she explained. "*It's Always Sunny in Philadelphia*?"

I shook my head. "Never seen it."

"Oh. Well, then let's cut that reference," she said. "We don't want to alienate younger viewers! And again . . ." She *clicked* and *clacked* a little more. "Now if you remember—"

The longer we filmed this, the more I realized there wasn't a whole lot of "real" in reality television.

"—when we last saw Laurel and Lucy together, there was a big blowup about the fact that Laurel had invited their housekeeper, Rose, to the wedding without first asking—"

"You forgot the part about how Lucy had invited Pete," Laurel added quickly.

"I was getting to that," Wendi assured her.

"I just think it's important that people have the entire story."

I was halfway through an eye roll before remembering that all of America would see me do it, so I stopped.

Wendi leaned in. "If you recall, Pete is Pete the Doorman," she whispered to the camera.

"I keep telling you guys," I said, "I didn't invite him! He misunderstood what I said!" At that, Dr. Maude gave a little meow, which, to anyone who understood Catese would know that it meant "Exactly!"

Over on Laurel's lap, Miss Piggy gave a low growl. It was as if even the cats had chosen sides. "You should let go of her," I said to Laurel. "It's a form of animal cruelty to hold them against their will like that. I think she wants to go back into my room."

"I'm not holding her against her will," she said. She lifted her hands up. "See?"

I waited for Miss Piggy to move, but she stayed put. Not only that, but she started purring. Loudly.

"I think Miss Piggy prefers an uncluttered environment," she added.

Okay, that was it. I had had enough about my messiness.

I stood up. "I think we should let Wendi be the judge of my mess—sorry, my *creative organization*."

Wendi's eyebrow went up. "You're finally going to let us go into your room?"

When we were coming up with the contract about the filming, one of the things I had insisted on was the fact that Wendi and her crew couldn't come in my room. It's not like I was embarrassed about it or anything, but I was afraid that some people in America—like, say, Laurel-types—wouldn't understand my particular brand of organization.

"Yes," I said as I led the group over. I opened the door a crack and peered in, checking to make sure there wasn't anything embarrassing on the floor, like a bra or a pair of underwear. Once I was sure the coast was clear, I opened the door. Dr. Maude ran in and tried to jump up on the bed but failed due to her coordination issues. "See? My room isn't messy," I said.

From the looks on the faces of Wendi and everyone else, they didn't look so convinced.

"Fine. Ask me where anything is, and I'll find it," I announced.

"How about . . . your cell phone?" Nikko suggested.

I marched over to my desk, swept aside the schoolbooks and pieces of notebook paper that covered it, and grabbed my phone. "One cell phone!" I announced proudly, as I held it up in the air.

"What about . . . your laptop?" Charles asked.

Striding over to the overstuffed purple and pink chair in the corner that was supposed to be used for reading but never was because of all the clothes that were piled on it, I rummaged underneath them and pulled it out. "One laptop!"

The crew looked at each other, impressed. Even Laurel looked surprised that I had been able to find it. "What about 'The Official Crush Log of the Girls at the Center for Creative Learning in New York, New York?'" she asked.

"What's 'The Official Crush Log of the Girls at the Center for Creative Learning in New York, New York'?" Wendi asked.

"Thanks, Laurel," I said under my breath as I felt my face get red. Now everyone in America was going to know about my logs? "It's just this place where everyone gets to list their local, long-distance-slash-vacation, and celebrity crushes."

As Wendi and her group looked at one another, I felt my head sink down into my shoulders, like a turtle going back into its shell. I waited for them to burst into laughter. Instead they all began to nod their heads and *hmmm* and *mmmm*.

"Honey, that is *so* cute!" Wendi peeped. "What a fantastic idea!"

My head began to rise up again. "You think so?"

"Oh *yes*. It's just darling," she replied. The rest of them nodded in agreement.

I was back to my normal height. "Thanks." I smiled.

"So where is it?" Laurel asked.

I walked over to my night table, which had a bunch of stuff piled on it in such a way that it looked like a mini Tower of Pisa. As I reached my hand into the middle of it and yanked, the group gasped, even more so when the pile stayed upright, kind of like when a magician pulled a tablecloth out without dumping over the plates. "It's right here," I said proudly.

"How'd you do that?" Wendi gasped.

I shrugged. "When you're a creatively organized person, you kind of have to learn how to do those types of things. Otherwise you really make a mess," I explained. "You want to see my advice notebook?" I asked.

They nodded.

"Great. It's right . . ." Uh-oh.

"So you don't know where it is?" Laurel asked smugly.

"Of course I do. It's . . ." Where was it? Finally, I remembered and walked over to my drawers, opening the one that held my socks. "Right here," I said, holding it up.

"In your sock drawer?" Laurel asked.

"Yeah. 'Cause the last thing I wrote down was about how important it is to wear comfortable shoes," I explained.

Nikko shrugged. "Makes sense to me."

"So you want to hear some of my advice?" I asked the group.

They nodded.

I thumbed through the pages. Where to start? With how to stop yourself from completely soaking your leg in winter by stepping into a snow puddle as you cross the street? (Make sure to tap around on the edges to see if it's solid or not before stepping.) What to do when you're talking to someone with really awful breath? (Just happen to arrange for a pack of gum to fall out of your bag right near their feet and when they pick it up to hand it to you, say, "Thanks so much. You're totally welcome to have a piece if you want.") It was all so good that to deny them any of the great advice that I had carefully put together felt wrong. I looked up at them. "I'll just start at the beginning," I said before clearing my throat. "*Important Pieces of Advice. By Lucy B. Parker,*" I read.

At first they seemed a little bored. (Personally, I thought that the bit I had gotten from Rose about using peanut butter to get gum out of your hair was pretty brilliant, but from the looks on their faces, they didn't agree.) But when I flipped to the chapter entitled "How to Get Along with Others … Especially When They're Being Super Annoying," they perked up.

"Wait—can you read that one again?" Charles asked. "The one about right and happy?"

"Sure," I said. "*When you're having an argument with someone—even if you're absolutely, positively sure what you're saying is correct, and know that you could prove it if they'd just let you Google it—think about this: Would you rather be right, or would you rather be happy?"* I read. *"Because sometimes being right, while it might make YOU happy, ends up making the other person very UNhappy, which therefore cancels out your happiness."*

"Huh. *Interesting,*" he said as he glanced at Wendi. "I know a few people in particular who could really benefit from keeping that in mind."

"And the one about the finger pointing?" Camilla asked.

I flipped back a few pages. *"Remember that when you point a finger at someone, there are three pointing back at you,"* I read. *"So if someone is doing something that really annoys you, chances are, you might be guilty of that yourself at times."*

"Oh, I just *love* that one," Wendi chirped. "It's utterly super."

Laurel looked at her watch. "It's time for me to go to the school for the blind to do some research. I thought maybe you'd like to get some footage of me there, Wendi."

Wendi turned to her. "Oh, honey—that sounds interesting, but it's kind of, you know, *really* depressing," she said. "And research has shown that if something is too depressing, viewers tend to change the channel." She turned back to me. "Lucy, you're just terrific at this advice stuff. I completely understand why they gave you your own column in the school newspaper."

"Thanks," I said. Now didn't seem like the right time, but once we were all done shooting, maybe I'd take

Beatrice's suggestion to see if Wendi might be interested in spinning me off into my own show. That's how Dr. Maude had gotten her start after appearing on a famous talk show host named Ophira's show a bunch of times.

"Well, what about afterward?" Laurel said. "When I'm practicing my synchronized swimming?" Feeling her character needed a hobby, the producers had made the screenwriter add in this whole thing about how, before she went blind, Jenny was training to go to the Olympics for synchronized swimming.

Wendi turned to Camilla. "What do you think?"

She wrinkled her nose. "Eh."

Wendi turned back to Laurel. "Honey, why don't you go do your thing and we'll just stay here with Lucy?" she said.

"Oh. Okay," she said, disappointed. "Well, have fun." She walked toward the door, trying to muster a smile. "I wish I could stay and hang out with you." But I could tell from the sound of her voice and the way that her eyes weren't smiling that she didn't mean it. That was covered in the section of the advice notebook entitled "When People Are Acting Weird." (Also in this section was *"When a parent is dating someone, and they say, 'Things are getting serious,' chances are, soon enough they'll be sitting you down to tell you they're getting married."* Followed by the advice, *"If a parent says they need to talk to you and then takes you to a restaurant to do it, make sure you pick one that has excellent desserts because they're going to feel so guilty for what it is that they're about to tell you that you'll probably get to order whatever you want.*")

When Laurel got to the door, she turned around. "What about shopping?!" she asked. "Do you want to film me shopping? Viewers love watching celebrities go shopping, don't they? I mean, I know *I* do."

Wendi nodded. "They sure do. And I *definitely* think we should do that—"

"What time?"

"—some other day," Wendy finished. She turned back to me. "Now back to your advice."

"Well, see you," Laurel mumbled as she slunk out.

I stood up. "Excuse me just a second," I said, and I ran after Laurel.

"Hey, are you okay?" I asked as I found her grabbing her cane and dark glasses near the front door.

"Of course I'm okay," she snapped, sounding very not okay. "Why wouldn't I be?"

I shrugged. "I don't know. I thought maybe because—"

But before I could say, "because of the fact that they're paying attention to me and not you," she had walked out and slammed the door behind her.

I opened the door. "I know I'm not a director or anything," I called after her, "but I don't think a blind person would move so fast!"

But the elevator doors had already closed behind her before I got the whole thing out.

chapter 8

Dear Dr. Maude,

I'm not sure what you're doing two weeks from now, but if things keep going the way they are then I have a feeling the wedding won't be happening. Which means I'll be in town, rather than at the Black Horse Inn in Vermont. So maybe we can hang out and take your dachshunds, Id and Ego, for a walk in Central Park. Also, I don't know if you like thrift stores and flea markets, but I've become an expert on the ones in New York, so I'd be happy to take you around to some. Oh, and in case you're worried about there being bedbugs in the stuff they sell there, you don't have to. I've bought a bunch of stuff, including cowboy boots, and I've never had a problem. Not even athlete's foot.

I have a feeling that if you DID read my letters you might think that I tend to exaggerate on account of the fact that a lot of things end up working out in my life. Like, say, me and Laurel becoming friends despite the Hat Incident. Or me beating Cristina Pollock in the election. However, a lot of things DON'T work out for me. Like, say, me getting my period. Or stopping my boobs from growing.

Which is why I'm not kidding when I say that I don't think this blended family thing is going to work. Mom walks around like she's plugged into an electrical outlet; Laurel only talks to me in one-word sentences (can a sentence only be one word?); and Alan spends all his time online checking the extended forecast to monitor any upcoming snowstorms that might interfere with the wedding. I just want things to go back to how they were, you know?

Any advice on that?

yours truly,
LUCY B. PARKER

Not knowing where else to turn, I decided to go to Northampton for advice. Not literally, but via Skype.

"I know you're bored just lying there in your crib staring at the ceiling most of the day, Zig," I said into the computer as Dr. Maude napped on my head, "but I have to tell you—I hope you're not in too much of a hurry to grow up because sometimes it's really not fun."

Most people would say it was my imagination, but at that, Ziggy made a thumbs-down sign with his tiny left hand.

"Exactly," I said. "But I have some news that might make you happy."

At that, he turned his head and cocked it to the side.

Maybe some people would've thought that was just a coincidence, but I knew better.

"The news is" —I leaned into the screen— "I might be coming to live with you."

At that he squealed so loud, it almost burst my eardrums.

"Ouch." I cringed. "Look, I know you're excited, but the squealing thing is *not* cool, Ziggy. In fact, it's really annoying. Did you pick that up from Marissa?" I demanded.

He giggled.

I sighed. "I knew I should have told Dad she wasn't the right babysitter for you."

Suddenly, Dad's face filled the screen. Actually, his ponytail filled the screen. Even though he was a guy, he wasn't very guy-like when it came to electronic stuff and never knew where to look on the webcam. "Lucy, what are you talking about you might be coming to live with us?"

I jumped. That was one of the problems with talking to a baby who didn't know how to talk yet. They couldn't say things like "Adult at ten o'clock."

"Dad, you were overlistening!" I cried.

"No, I wasn't," he replied. "The door was open, and at the exact moment that I was walking by, I got a cramp in my leg and had to stop to massage it."

I rolled my eyes. That was the oldest excuse in the book. When you were an expert overlistener like I was, you knew these things. "So how are you?" I asked, changing the subject. "Any interesting photo shoots lately? Ooh—did Mr. Campbell hire you again to do Sam dressed as Rudolph, the Red-Nosed Reindeer?!"

Dad was what they called a "fine art photographer"—meaning he took pictures of things that were sometimes so blurry you couldn't even tell what they were (I'm not sure why that was considered art, but it was). Because people didn't always want pictures of blurry objects, or hands, or the corner of a bridge that was blown up so big that you could no longer tell it was a bridge, he sometimes took family portraits to make extra money. And, around the holidays, he took pet portraits that people then used for their holiday cards, like Sam the Dalmatian as Rudolph. Those were my favorite. Back when I lived in Northampton I used to be Dad's assistant for those shoots.

"Don't change the subject," he said as his nostrils filled the screen.

"Ew—Dad! Can you please move back?!" I cried.

As he moved the laptop back, I could finally see him normally. Ever since having Ziggy, he looked so ... *dad*-like. Not Alan-dad-like, meaning bald with unfaded jeans that were too high at the waist and too short at the feet. But he *had* cut his hair a bit, so his ponytail wasn't as long. He looked like a man trying to grow a ponytail rather than someone who had had one his whole life.

"Is this better?" he asked.

I nodded. "Hey, so how was that special you and Sarah were about to watch on the Discovery Channel the other night?" I asked, still trying to change the subject. "The one about how following an ayurvedic diet can help you live to 117?"

At that, Ziggy made a raspberry sound. I knew from Sarah that ayurveda was this Indian way of eating for your body type. And I also knew from her that according to the people who practiced it, pizza and ice cream weren't considered good for anyone's body type, which immediately made it something I wasn't interested in hearing more about, even though Sarah thought I should follow it because it would help me with my oily skin.

"It was interesting," he said. "But you're still changing the subject."

I took a deep breath. "Dad, this whole wedding thing is a total mess," I blurted out. As I told him all about The Change, I felt my stomach begin to unknot. Maybe there *was* something to this whole communication thing my parents were so big on. I told him how Laurel and I were fighting; about the running tally I was keeping of how many times Mom called her "honey" and "sweetie" versus me (Laurel—22, me—19); and about how every time a person used the word *wedding* in front of Mom she got all freaked out and looked like she was going to throw up.

"Ah. So it's happening again," he said as he picked Ziggy up and started walking him around the room.

"What's happening again?" I asked, confused.

Now that Ziggy was out of his cage—aka his crib—he kept lunging at the computer with his hands held out as if he wanted me to pick him up. And every time he did that, I found myself leaning forward to the computer screen with my arms flying out as if I was going to do it.

"Well, let's just say your mother gets a little . . . *uncomfortable* when it comes to the c-word."

"What's the c-word?" I asked.

"Commitment," he replied. "See, once she's actually married, she's fine. But that window in between the deciding to get married and the wedding can be a little . . . *challenging* for everyone around her."

"By 'challenging', do you mean that she's cranky and has no sense of humor and barely ever smiles?"

He nodded. "Yup. That would be what I'm talking about. Has she started eating sugar?"

I nodded, surprised. "Yeah."

"What about soda? Has she started in on that?"

I thought about it. Now that he mentioned it . . .

"Back then she couldn't stop downing root beer," he went on.

Oh my God. There had been an empty bottle of root beer in the recycling can! I couldn't believe my mother had been drinking soda. My entire life she had been going on and on about how it ruined the enamel on your teeth. Once, during the current events portion of one of our official family dinners, she had passed around an article about how when Coca-Cola was poured on the hood of a car, it ate away at the paint. ("If it can do that to a car, Lucy, just think of what it's doing to the inside of your stomach.") The only time I was allowed to drink soda (in front of them, at least) was very special occasions, like when they were about to tell me something that was going to change my life forever: they were getting divorced, they wanted us to move to New York, or they were about to have a new baby.

His face clouded over as he remembered the past. "It was bad, Lucy. Really bad. In fact, Deanna and I started talking about doing an intervention."

Deanna was Mom's BFF from Northampton. I knew from reality shows what interventions were. They were when you tried to get people to stop doing bad things, like drugs or hoarding. All the people who loved them— like their families and their BFFs—got together and surprised them and told them why what they were doing was so bad for them and they were going to die if they didn't stop.

I couldn't believe this was my *mom* he was talking about. "And then what happened?"

"Well, after the soda came the bad TV," he replied. "She'd stay up until all hours of the night watching sitcoms, game shows ... even infomercials."

"But Mom barely ever watches TV," I said. "She

reads." Mostly she liked magazines like *The New Yorker*, which had very tiny print and no pictures other than cartoons that only adults found funny.

He shook his head sadly. "Not back then," he said. He sighed "I can still see it. All those piles of unread *Newsweeks* and *Vanity Fairs*. And when she did read, it was things like the *National Enquirer*."

Okay, this was just weird. Mom hated those gossip magazines. Especially after we moved in with Laurel and she saw firsthand how they printed total lies, like how Laurel was actually an alien.

"Well, watch out for that," he said. "That's a sure sign she's going to blow."

Okay, this was not good. In fact, this was starting to sound very, very bad.

"But like I said, it's only temporary." He smiled. "I can tell you from experience, once the wedding's over with, she'll go back to being her old self."

If we actually *made* it to the wedding.

"Think of it as a . . . growth opportunity," he said with a smile.

I sighed. I had had so many growth opportunities over the last year I felt like I should have been seven feet tall instead of four feet eleven. "Dad?"

"Yeah?

I flopped back on the bed. "I wouldn't mind staying this size for a while."

He laughed again. "Yeah, well, I'm afraid that's not an option."

I sat up. "But what am I supposed to do about Laurel?"

"What do you mean?"

"Well, I mean it's pretty obvious that she doesn't want to be friends anymore, let alone fristers."

"Lucy, this Change thing—it scares you a little, right?"

I crossed my arms and turned away from the computer. "I never said it *scared* me."

At that, Ziggy let out another raspberry. It was *crazy* how smart he was for a baby. Forget about trying to pull the whole Santa Claus thing over on him in a few years.

"Okay, fine," I said stubbornly. "So maybe it scares me a little bit."

"Which makes complete sense," Dad said. "seeing that you're a human being and not a robot, and human beings are not huge fans of change. So if you're scared, what makes you think that Laurel's not scared, too, and that's why she's acting like this?"

"But Laurel's not human," I blurted out.

"She's not?"

"Well, yes, she's human, but it's different for her."

"How come?"

"Because she's the most popular girl in the world!"

"Lucy, after everything you know about Laurel, is that what you really think?"

I sighed. "I guess not."

The thing was, I didn't know what I thought anymore. Everyone was acting so nutty around me that I couldn't help being that way, too.

No one in the family was wild about the idea of Wendi and her crew showing up at the crack of dawn to film us getting ready for our day, but her hope was to get some footage of us "unplugged." Laurel was already at the studio, so it was just Mom and Alan and me.

I was so tired that I poured orange juice on top of my cereal instead of milk. I had stayed up late spying on Mom, watching as she sat on the couch late into the night downing fistfuls of Reese's Pieces while watching *Celebrity Rehab Top Model Search* and flipping through *In Touch with Style*.

"I hate to eat and run," Mom said as she finished off a Skinny Cow mint ice cream sandwich. *For breakfast.* (Even I didn't do that.) "But I really need to get through the episodes of *Shipwrecked!* I DVRed. The finale is tonight and I want to be all caught up."

Okay, not good. *Shipwrecked!* was the lowest of the low when it came to reality programs. They took a group of people and put them on a fancy boat only to then sail them into a storm somewhere until they got shipwrecked and were forced to live on a desert island for one month, with weekly weigh-ins. There were contests about who could make the most creative meals out of berries and plants, and who made the best outfits out of stuff they found washed up on shore. Even Alice, who loved reality programs (the cheesier the better), didn't watch that one.

"Honey, what are you doing watching *Shipwrecked!*?" asked Alan, baffled.

Mom reached into her back pocket and took out a York Peppermint Pattie and unwrapped it and popped it into her mouth. Again, even I tended to stay away from chocolate until at least nine a.m. "What's wrong with *Shipwrecked!*?" she asked defensively. "You know, Alan, there's more to life than just news programs and documentaries about World War Two."

"I know that, honey, it's just that it's so not . . . *you*," he replied. "And what are you doing eating junk food?"

"Why is everyone getting on me about what I'm eating?" she cried. "I'm allowing myself a little treat—is that really so bad? So what if I have to fit into a dress in"—she looked at her watch—"six days, twenty-two hours, and forty-three seconds. It'll be fine!" she cried. "Or you know what? Maybe it won't be fine and I'll just wear . . . a *caftan*!" She shoved another pattie in her mouth. "Maybe *you* should try eating some junk food once in a while," Mom went on. "Maybe it would help with that little scheduling problem of yours."

"Scheduling *problem*? It's not a problem," Alan said. "It's . . . a lifestyle choice." His faced dropped. "I thought you liked it."

Mom snorted. "I think the 'choice' part was gone a long time ago."

"*Someone* in this family has to be a little organized and come up with a schedule," Alan said. "Otherwise, we'd be living in complete . . . *chaos.*"

"Oh, so what you're saying is that I'm not organized at all?" Mom demanded.

"If we're talking about the fact that every time we try and leave it takes an extra three to five minutes because you can't find your keys even though the first thing I did when you moved in was put up a little hook by the door with a sign that says 'Rebecca's Keys,' then, yes, I'm saying that maybe that's something you want to look at," he snapped.

"You know, back in Northampton, there was no hook and I got through life just fine!" Mom cried.

Wendi turned to Nikko. "Please tell me you're getting this," she whispered.

He nodded. "Oh yeah."

"I didn't realize you were so much happier in Northampton," Alan said.

"I didn't *say* I was happier in Northampton," Mom corrected.

"Well, you sure are acting like it lately!" Alan said angrily.

Okay, whoa. Alan barely ever got angry. Nervous, yes. Stressed out, absolutely. But angry?

"And you sure do sound angry!" Mom retorted.

"Maybe I am," he snapped.

"Maybe I am, too," she snapped back.

He stood up. "Maybe this breakfast should be adjourned so everyone can take a time-out!"

"Maybe that's a good idea!" she agreed, standing up as well.

"Fine!" he said, stomping toward his office.

"I was going to say that first," she said, stomping toward the bedroom.

That left me and Dr. Maude (lapping up the orange juice left in my cereal bowl) sitting at the table with a very surprised TV crew.

"So, ah, I could go get my advice notebook and read you guys some more advice, if you want," I said, trying to save what seemed to be a completely unsavable situation.

From the way the crew started to pack up their stuff, I was going to take it as a no.

"Or not," I said as they left the room.

"I don't know why we're even bothering to do this," I said to Blair that afternoon as we sat in his room while he pushed a lot of buttons on his computer that took the photo files I had sent him and started to make them into a slide show.

"How about . . . because slide shows don't just magically appear?" he asked. "Especially ones that resemble award-winning music videos."

I rolled my eyes as I reached for one of the fried plantains that I had smuggled out of my apartment. I was always telling Rose that they were so good she totally could've opened a store, or at least one of those food trucks, and sold them all over Manhattan. "You know what I mean. Because this whole wedding might not even happen after this morning!"

He shook his head. "You girls. You're such ... *drama queens.*"

"I am not!" I cried. "Alice is, and my friend Marissa *definitely* is, but I'm like the *opposite* of one."

"Oh yeah? Then how come you're all *Oh no! This wedding is totally not going to happen and Laurel hates me and my life is over!*" he cried in a very high-pitched, very non-me voice.

"Well, all of that is true," I said calmly.

Now he was the one who rolled his eyes. "I rest my case." He pointed to a picture on the screen of Laurel and me from our day at the Holyoke Mall when we had played The World's Ugliest Outfit. "This sure doesn't look like two people who hate each other," he said.

He clicked on another photo, this one taken in one of our IBSs to the Target in Riverdale, which was way up on the 1 train in the Bronx. "She sure doesn't look like she hates you here."

I smiled sadly as I looked at the way she had her arms thrown around my neck and was leaning in to plant a big kiss on my cheek. "Of course she doesn't,"

I said. "That's because I had just showed her Target's Merona line. They have awesome stuff." I thought it was pretty cool that a huge star like Laurel, who could afford anything she wanted (even though she was always being given free clothes by the biggest designers anyway), now preferred clothes from Target.

Blair wrinkled his nose. "You girls and your clothes. I will never understand that."

I shrugged. "What? It's like the female equivalent to computer stuff."

"I guess you're right," he said. "Look, here's the deal— sometimes you just have be the bigger person—"

Again with this bigger person stuff?!

"—and just suck it up because some people are, you know, not as cool as you," he went on. "Believe me, I have to do that all the time."

"How can you say Laurel's not cool?" I asked. "She's on the top of every cool list in every magazine."

He shrugged. "So?" He looked down at the ground. "She's not as cool as you."

Although it took everything in me, I managed to keep my jaw semi-shut even though it wanted to flap open really, really wide. Had Blair Lerner-Moskovitz just said that I, Lucy B. Parker, was cooler than Laurel Moses? I almost asked him to repeat it but stopped myself.

"I'm sure Laurel's somewhat cool or else you wouldn't have pictures like this," he said, pointing to one of us on a red carpet.

I smiled. "That was from a movie premiere in L.A."
I left out the part that it also happened to be the night I
had my first kiss, with Connor Forrester, in the parking
lot of a hamburger place.

He squinted. "Why are you wearing that weird-
looking scarf on your head?"

"It's a turban," I replied. "They happen to be very hip
in some fashion circles." I also left out the part that I had
had to borrow it from Lady Countess Annabel Ashcroft
de Winter von Taxi, a famous actress, because she turned
my hair blue as she was helping me get dressed.

"Whatever," he said. "But even if Laurel's famous and
has her own TV show, that doesn't mean she's any better
than you. She's just a human being."

Had he been talking to my dad or what?

"So what you're saying is that I should go apologize
even though I didn't do anything?" I asked.

"I'm not saying you should apologize," he said, "I'm
just saying that maybe if you just go in and talk to her
like things are normal, then they can be again."

I shook my head. "I don't know."

"What do you have to lose?" he asked. "It's not like
your way is working."

He did have a point.

It was a good thing that Blair had said that he wasn't
going to help me until I at least went up and gave it a

try, because when I did get back up to Laurel's room, she needed some serious help.

"So Laurel," Wendi was saying as she *clicked* and *clacked* her way across Laurel's floor, "are there any. . . . *regrets* about becoming famous as such a young age?"

I could see Laurel sit up straighter. "What do you mean?"

"Well, you know, when you're famous, it takes away any ability to be a normal person."

Uh-oh. Laurel had a lot of issues about missing out on being a normal person. Just recently she had gone on this normal-person kick and insisted on doing all these normal-person things like go to American Girl Place. Which, when you're a huge star instead of a normal person, means you get mobbed by crowds and the manager gets mad because a lot of dolls end up getting beheaded in the process.

Laurel shrugged. "I don't know. I like to think I'm pretty normal." She sat up straighter. "I've been to American Girl Place and everything," she said proudly.

I cringed. She had just admitted that on national television? Seriously?

"Oh. How cute," Wendi said. "But even when you're around other kids your age don't you always feel like . . . I don't know . . . there's a pane of glass between you and them?"

I could see Laurel's bottom lip begin to jiggle a bit. "No."

"Really? You don't feel as if . . . I don't know . . . as

glamorous as all the premieres and award shows may be, at the end of the day, when you get into your bed to go to sleep, you're acutely aware that although you may play a regular girl on TV, you're just ... *not* normal?"

With that, Wendi got what she wanted because Laurel's eyes began to get misty. At the moment, she didn't look like a superstar, or a know-it-all older sister, or even like some midlevel popular girl in some junior high in Illinois. She looked like I had felt on my first day of school in New York when I was the New Girl and didn't have anyone to sit with at lunch. Or the day when my ex-BFFs Rachel and Missy dumped me right before sixth grade started. Which is to say, she looked totally and completely ... alone.

It was so hard to watch that it almost made *me* cry, too. Sure, we hadn't been getting along lately, but for better or worse, Laurel was and always would be my frister—whether our parents got married or not. And the number one rule for fristers is that they stand up for each other—even when they're technically kind-of, sort-of in a fight.

"She is, too!" I cried, barging into the room. "Maybe she's on the super-organized end of the normal scale, but speaking as someone who is abnormally normal, I promise you—Laurel Moses is definitely more normal than superstarry."

Laurel turned to me. "You really think so?" she asked shyly.

"Totally," I replied. I turned back to Wendi. "Cristina Pollock is more superstarry than Laurel!" I blurted.

"Who's Cristina Pollock?" Wendi asked.

Whoops. Maybe I shouldn't have said that. "She's um...actually, maybe you can cut that last line...anyway, who she is is not important. What *is* important is that Laurel is funny and nice and likes to shop at Target and eats the frosting off her cupcakes before taking a bite of the actual cake part—just like any normal girl," I said. "And to say that she's not normal would be a total lie, which means you might get *sued.*"

At the word *sued,* Camilla tapped Wendi on the shoulder. "Let's move on from this particular topic, shall we?"

Wendi stepped in front of the camera and leaned into it. "As you'll remember, the last few days have been fraught with tension here in the Parker-Moses house—especially between superstar Laurel Moses and her soon-to-be official stepsister, Lucy Parker—"

"Excuse me," I called out. "But (a) it's Lucy B. Parker, and (b) we prefer the term *frister*, not stepsister"—I turned to Laurel— "Unless something's changed that I don't know about and you'd rather be stepsisters."

"Why would you say that?" she asked.

I shrugged. "I don't know."

"I never thought anything changed," she replied. "I thought *you* thought something had changed."

"That's because I thought *you* thought something

162

had changed!" I cried. "It's just that you were saying I was messy, and then you told the story about the Hat Incident—"

"I told it because I thought it was funny. And because it shows how far we've come since the first time we met," she replied. "It's not like I told it to embarrass you."

"Well, that's how it felt," I said. "And then you got all weird when these guys were talking to me about my advice notebook."

She looked down at the floor. "I know I did," she said quietly. "I guess I was ... I don't know ... a little jealous."

"Jealous? Of what?"

She shrugged. "That you were getting all the attention." She looked up at me. "I sat there listening to you, and I realized how great you are. And it made me feel so ... average."

"Average?!" I cried. "Laurel, you're the most famous girl in the entire world!"

"What about all that stuff you said about her being normal?" Nikko asked.

"She is, but you can be normal and famous at the same time," I replied.

He thought about it. "I guess you can."

"Actually, this week she's not the most famous girl in the world," Wendi corrected. "This week that four-year-old girl who fell down the well and was trapped there for three days is. She's on the cover of all the magazines." She snapped her fingers. "Charles, make a note for me to get in touch with that girl's parents and see if we can book her for a show."

"Well, the other fifty-one weeks of the year she is," I said. I turned back to Laurel. "Laurel, you're totally not average. Even if you weren't famous, you wouldn't be average. Don't take this the wrong way, but you're too ... *weird* to be average."

"Really?" she asked hopefully.

I nodded.

"And then I got mad at myself for feeling jealous because I know that you have to deal with me being in the spotlight all the time."

I shrugged. "Yeah, but it's okay. I've gotten used to it by now." Sometimes it's not until words leave your mouth that you realize how you really feel about something. The truth was, being the frister of the most famous girl in the world *was* okay, and I *had* gotten used to it. Mostly because I knew from living with Laurel that no matter how put together someone looked on the outside (or how clean their room was), that wasn't necessarily who they were on the inside. On the inside, they could be scared and lonely. And once you realized that about people, suddenly there was nothing to be nervous about. Like them getting all the attention while you were left behind.

Laurel reached for my hand. "Can I say something? I know it's going to sound really lame and dorky, but I don't care."

"What?"

"I think *you're* the superstar in the family. Not me,"
she said. "And not just because you give great advice, or
wear lots of color. It's because—"

I sighed. "Let me guess. It's my all-around...*Lucyness*."
She nodded.

My Lucyness was something that Mom had brought
up a few months back when I was talking to her about
being afraid that now that we had moved in with Alan
and Laurel, she was going to end up loving Laurel
more than me. (Which, with the amount of *honey*s and
*sweetie*s Laurel was getting, might actually be the case.)
Even after asking Mom to explain it to me a bunch of
times, I still wasn't sure what it meant, but apparently
it had to do with everything that made me me. Like
my love of color. And my sneaker and hat collections.
And my logs. Even the stuff that I wasn't proud of and
thought was embarrassing, like my coordination issue
and my bloversharing problem—those, too, were part of
my Lucyness. Not only were they part of it, but according
to Mom, they were some of the best parts because they
made me human.

Personally, I found the whole being-human thing
very embarrassing at times, but the truth was when
other people were being human, that's when I felt closest
to them and loved them the most. Like how Laurel was
admitting that she was worried that she was average.
That was totally human, because I worried about that

exact same thing. And when she said it, my chest got warm, around where my heart was, and it made me feel really close to her.

Wendi shoved her face in front of the camera. "People, what you are witnessing is not scripted like other quote-unquote reality shows out there," she whispered. "This is *real*. This is *from the heart*." She grabbed both of us and pulled us toward her, hugging us tight. "This is two fristers *bonding*." Her eyes filled with tears. "I never had a sister," she sniffed. "I always wanted one. Instead I grew up an only child—"

Nikko looked down at the camera. "Uh-oh—I think the battery's running low. I'm going to have to turn this off for a second. Sorry," he announced, winking at me and Laurel.

Laurel and I looked at each other and giggled. It was nice to have someone to exchange looks with again.

Now that Laurel and I were back on track, I had one more thing I needed to do before I could get back to my toast: Get Mom and Alan back to their we-get-along-so-well-that-at-times-it-can-be-nauseating-to-all-who-have-to-watch-it state.

Which was why I called an emergency family meeting.

As I stood in front of the family (and TV crew), I took a deep breath. Could I do this? Could I get Mom to stop eating all the candy in sight and Mom and Alan to stop fighting so that things could go back to normal?

"You can do this, Lucy," Laurel whispered, reaching up and squeezing my hand. "I know you can."

That's something that happened with fristers—you became a little bit psychic around them. I smiled at her as I squeezed back. Maybe my parents were about to get divorced before they even got married, but even if that happened, I'd always have Laurel, because fristers were forever.

I marched over and stood in front of Mom and Alan, who were sitting on the couch with their arms crossed in front of their chests. "Okay, you guys. The reason I've called an emergency family meeting is because this wedding thing has gotten completely out of control." As Mom opened her mouth, I put my hand up. "Yes. I said *wedding*. Because that's what it is. Not a nice party. Not a gathering of immediate family. It's a wedding. Where two people promise to do their best to stick together through thick and thin."

I heard a sniffle behind me. "Oh, that's such a lovely way of putting it," Wendi whispered.

"Even if the other person sometimes annoys them with agendas and lists," I went on.

"Well, I know how *that* feels," Mom said.

I turned to her. "*Or* with the fact that they lose their keys all the time and freak out and get all snappy."

"I think we *all* know how that feels," Alan replied.

Mom turned red.

"Mom, when I was talking to Dad the other day, he mentioned that you had a little bit of trouble with the c-word."

"What's the c-word?" Alan asked.

"*Commitment*," I replied.

As soon as the word left my mouth, Mom looked like she was melting into her seat. It was like watching the Wicked Witch of the West being doused with water.

"He said that right before you guys got married, you were doing this same sort of thing," I explained. "The junk food...the bad TV...the soda—"

Alan turned to Mom. "There's been *soda* involved?"

She shrugged. "Maybe a *little* soda." When she saw Laurel's right eyebrow go up, she sighed. "Okay, fine. A lot. There's been a lot of soda." She sighed again. "Okay, fine, before my first wedding, I guess I got a little ... *nervous*. And the food and the TV and the soda...that was just all stuff to, you know, calm me down."

"But soda has caffeine in it," Laurel said. "Wouldn't that make you more nervous?"

"That's a very good point," I agreed.

"Well, yes, but when you're in that much of a state, you're really not thinking about that sort of thing," Mom said.

"But why were you nervous?" asked Laurel.

Mom shrugged. "I don't know. Because getting married is so...permanent."

"Actually, it's not," Nikko said. "My mom's been married and divorced four times."

"The only thing really permanent is death," Laurel added.

"Except if you're a Buddhist," I corrected.

"Are you saying you don't want to get married?" Alan asked anxiously.

She grabbed his hand. "No! Of course not!" she cried. "Honey, there's nothing I want more than to marry you." She looked at the three of us sheepishly. "I guess I've been a little hard to live with lately, huh?"

"A *little*?" I asked.

"Okay. A lot," Mom replied. "I'm sorry, you guys. I really am." Her eyes got all wet and she turned to Alan. "Alan Edward Moses, if you're not busy this weekend, would you consider going to a wedding with me?"

Now his eyes got all misty. "I would love nothing more," he said with a smile.

As they kissed, Laurel and I looked away.

"I guess things are officially back to normal," I whispered to Laurel.

chapter 9

Dear Dr. Maude,

I just want you to know that all the hours I've spent watching your show have really paid off.

Today I was able to get Mom and Alan to stop fighting and make up. In fact, things went so well that it ended in a group hug! (I've noticed that those don't happen that often on your show anymore.) Not only is Mom no longer freaking out about the wedding—she's actually excited about it. To the point where we're even allowed to call it a wedding, which is good because the other stuff was a real mouthful.

I'd like to think that if you had seen me in action you would've been proud. And thanks to Blair's suggestion, I ended up being the bigger person and making up with Laurel so now we're back to being fristers. I mean, we never really stopped being fristers during that whole sort-of fight, but we weren't exactly being fristerly to each other, if that makes sense.

Anyway, I don't really have time to be chatting at the moment, because now that I'm positive there's going to be a wedding I need to get my video toast finished. I just thought you'd want to know I put your advice to good use. Not, you know, any sort of advice that you came up with for me personally because you never write me back, but the advice that any stranger could get for free by watching your show.

yours truly,
LUCY B. PARKER

"OMIGOD, I CAN'T BELIEVE THE WEDDING IS THIS WEEKEND!" Marissa shrieked into the computer during our weekly Triple S.

I leaned back. "You mentioned that already, Marissa," I said. "Four times." Just then Dr. Maude jumped on my lap and started hissing at the screen.

"HI, DR. MAUDE!" she shouted. "IT'S ME, MARISSA, YOUR AUNT!"

At that, Dr. Maude tried to bite the screen.

"So now that your mom's done being weird do you think I can come to the wedding?" she asked.

I shook my head. "Nope. She still wants to keep it small."

Just then, Mom walked in with my clean laundry and started placing it on my bed. "Who are you Skyping with?"

"You don't really want to—" I started to say.

"HI, MRS. PARKER! IT'S ME, MARISSA!" she yelled.

"Hi, Marissa. How are you, honey?"

Wow. Mom was *really* in a good mood. I wasn't sure Marissa's own mother had ever called her "honey."

"Oh, I'm fine I guess," Marissa said. She gave a long, hard sigh. "Other than not being invited to the wedding, even though I know from Beatrice's Twitter feed that *she* gets to go."

Uh-oh. I did not like where this was going. Not one single bit.

"I mean, I could understand if it were just family," Marissa went on. "Even though I'm *kind* of family. Because I'm Ziggy's babysitter and all. But now that friends are being invited . . ."

I slunk down in my chair. I know Mom was in a much better mood lately, but she wasn't in such a good mood that she'd—

"Well, you know, now that we've decided not to make it just family, why don't you join us, Marissa?" Mom asked.

I put my face in my hands. Apparently, yes. She was in such a good mood she was going to invite Marissa to the wedding.

The shriek that came out of Marissa's mouth was so loud it could have woken up dead people. "OMIGODOMIGODOMIGOD!" she yelled. "THAT WOULD BE THE COOLEST THING EVER!"

I turned to Mom. "You know, that *would* be cool, but I don't think Marissa's mom would let her take the bus by herself," I said. "Plus, this place is in the middle of nowhere. They might not even *have* buses that go there."

"She can ride with either Dad or Deanna," Mom replied. Now that the wedding wasn't just limited to family, Deanna was also coming. My grandmother, however, was going to be on a cruise, so she wouldn't make it.

"Ziggy and I are going to have soooo much fun together in the car!" Marissa yelled.

That poor kid. I really hoped that he wouldn't hold this against me when he got older.

"I should go," she went on. "I have, like, nine million things I need to do before Saturday! See ya!" she yelled as she disconnected from Skype.

Mom and I looked at each other. "She is a *little* like family," she said.

I sighed. I guess she was. For better or for worse.

"Are you *sure* we didn't make a wrong turn?" Alan asked anxiously that Wednesday as we drove up to the Black Horse Inn. Everyone else was coming on Friday, but Alan thought it would be nice for us to have some private bonding time as a family beforehand. Well, as private as could be when a camera crew was following you around.

For the last two hours, all we had seen were miles and miles of empty fields. Empty except for when there were horses. And cows. And, at one point, a three-legged dog that I begged Mom and Alan to stop and let me take a picture of so I could send it in to the MostInspirationalPets.com website and maybe win a years' worth of Purina Puppy Chow, even though we didn't have a puppy and couldn't get one because of Mom's allergies. (They said no.)

"Nope. This is the right way. You heard Queen Elizabeth: '*Continue on Route 2 for 75.4 miles*,'" Mom said in a fake English accent.

"Yes, but sometimes Queen Elizabeth is wrong," Alan replied. That was the name that Laurel and I had given the woman on the GPS who called out directions, because of her English accent.

"Honey, we're going the right way," Mom said. She dug out a brochure from her bag that had a picture of an old farmhouse and a smiling couple standing next to a big basket of apples. "I told you the place was a little out of way. It says right here:—*With its rural charm and hospitality, the Black Horse Inn provides an oasis of tranquility away from the pressures of the modern world.*"

"Tranquility's great, but what if there's an emergency? I haven't seen a sign for a hospital for the last hour," he said. "What if someone gets stung by something?"

Central Park was as far into nature as Alan liked to go and that was only just across the street from our apartment.

"Sweetheart, I keep telling you. It's winter. There are

no bugs. So no one is going to get stung by anything and no one is going to need to go to the hospital," Mom said firmly. "Just relax and enjoy the beauty."

"But there *is* cable, right?" asked Laurel anxiously. MTV was airing a special that night called *Inside the Mind (and Crib) of Austin Mackenzie* that Laurel was dying to see. She had DVRed it (and then checked it five times to make sure it was set correctly), but didn't want to wait three whole days until we got back home to watch it, even though she'd be seeing him in the flesh in two days.

"I'm sure there's cable," Mom said. "Though I'd love to see if anyone in this family can go more than five hours without it."

"And there's Internet, right?" I asked. I wouldn't want Dr. Maude to finally e-mail me back and then get her feelings hurt that I didn't e-mail her back for days. Although maybe then she'd know how *I* felt.

"Yes, it has Internet," Mom sighed. "But this is our *wedding*. A time for us to spend quality time together and talk about how much we all mean to each other."

Or go stir-crazy from too much together time.

Two hours and many fields later we were standing on the porch of a sweet-looking farmhouse.

"Are you sure this is it?" Alan asked.

Mom pointed to the sign. "It does say the Black Horse Inn."

"I know, but it's just so . . . in the middle of nowhere," he replied.

Laurel began walking around the house.

"Laurel, honey, watch out for plants—you don't want to get poison ivy."

"I don't see a satellite dish," Laurel said.

I looked down at my iTouch. "And there's no signal up here."

Before Alan could go nuts like I knew he would (he got antsy when he was in an elevator and his BlackBerry wasn't working), Wendi and her crew pulled up in their SUV. As the passenger door opened, she stumbled out, looking like she had walked through a wind tunnel. "Nikko, as soon as we get back to the city, I'm signing you up for a driving course," she announced.

"What?" he asked. "So I was going a few miles above the speed limit."

"Ninety-five in a sixty-five mile zone is not a *few* miles," she snapped.

The front door opened and out came an old couple wearing matching Black Horse Inn sweatshirts. "Welcome! Welcome!" the man boomed. "I'm Bill Wilson."

"And I'm Lois," the woman said. "We were starting to wonder if all this fresh country air had scared you off and sent you right back home."

"Not yet," Alan said under his breath.

"Excuse me, but you do have a TV, right?" Laurel asked politely.

"Oh sure," Bill said. "Lois loves those English mystery shows on the public television station."

"And Bill's a big fan of *Bowling for Beer*," Lois said.

"Cable?" I asked.

Bill shook his head. "Nope. Got rid of that a little while back," he said. He turned to Lois. "When was that, honey?"

She thought about it. "1987, I think."

I thought about pointing out the fact that maybe they should've thought about updating their website so that it was more in line with this particular century, but decided against it.

Bill came bounding down the steps. For an old person, he moved really fast and carried our two heaviest bags in one hand right up the stairs without saying, "Oh, my back!" like most old people I knew said. Maybe it was all the farm work that I had a feeling people in Vermont did on a daily basis . Lois grabbed the other two bags like they weighed nothing. "Come along—lucky for you the afternoon snacks are still sitting out," she said.

"Oh, you don't want to miss Lois's snacks," Bill chuckled. "They're *dee-lish*!"

My stomach growled as images of brownies and Toll House chocolate chip cookies and Red Velvet cupcakes started bubbling to the surface. Between being so old and living in the middle of nowhere without cable, I bet Lois had spent lots of time perfecting all her recipes.

Or not. In my book, slices of apple with little squares of Vermont cheddar cheese were not considered dee-lish snacks. In fact, they weren't even considered snacks unless you were stuck on a desert island with your only other food options being leaves or berries that may or may not have been poisonous.

"This apple is very delicious," I said politely as I nibbled away, anxious to get to our room so I could break out some real snacks. Luckily, I had smuggled a bag of Uncle Eddie's vegan chocolate-chip cookies, some chocolate-covered banana chips, and some chocolate-covered apricots in my bag in case of emergency. (I was proud of myself for bringing so much fruit.)

"Glad you like it," Bill said, "'cause you're going to be eating a lot of them over the next few days." He chuckled. "When you've got an apple orchard, you can't let the fruit go to waste. Good thing they freeze so well. Lois is somewhat of a gourmet when it comes to apples."

"Oh, Bill," she said, swatting him on the arm. "You know how I feel when you boast like that."

"Well, now, it's the truth," he replied. He turned to us.

"I keep telling her she could fill a cookbook with all the different ways she knows how to use them. You'll see."

And we sure did. Dinner that night was baked chicken with braised apples, broccoli with applesauce ("First time Lois brought it to the table I thought to myself, 'What the hay?' but then I realized my bride knew what she was doing!"), and apple fritters dusted with powdered sugar.

"Well, this sure is a lot of fiber," Mom said, holding her stomach after dinner. Mine let out a very long, angry gurgle. We had learned about fiber in health class recently. Apparently, too much of it could make you really gassy. I was jealous that Wendi and her crew were at the local Pizza Hut near the Holiday Inn they were staying at. In Vermont, apparently "local" meant forty-five minutes away.

"Anyone want seconds on the fritters?" Lois asked.

We all patted our stomachs at the same time and politely said no.

"Best to take the time to digest," Lois agreed, "so you're good and ready for the apple cider apple French toast in the morning."

Even for someone like me who loved French toast, the idea of more apples made me wish for something boring like eggs.

Without cable, our TV-viewing options were limited

to some boring show on the PBS channel about maids in an English manor or a show about quilting, which is why Laurel and I decided to go to bed. At seven thirty. Which I hadn't done since I was like five.

"What's that noise?" I whispered after we pushed the twin beds together and were huddled under the blankets. The room was really cute. That is, if you liked lace doilies and framed pictures of people made out of what else but . . . apples.

"What noise?" Laurel whispered back. "I don't hear anything."

"That's what I mean. It's so . . . *quiet*." I had gotten so used to falling asleep with the sound of honking and sirens that all this stillness was creepy. It was like any minute the closet door was going to open up and a killer wearing an Elmo mask (like the guy in a horror script I had once read for Laurel) was going to jump out.

"I think lots of quiet when you sleep is good for you, though," Laurel said, yawning.

"Okay," I said. "Well, good night."

"Good night."

A half hour later I was still awake. Part of it was making sure that if the killer jumped out of the closet I could protect myself, but part of it was thinking about The Change. Sure, things *seemed* like they were okay again, but what if it was just an illusion and once the ceremony happened, The Change really happened?

"Laurel? Are you sleeping?" I said in a voice that was so loud that even if she was sleeping, she sure wouldn't be for long.

"Hmpf?" she muttered.

"I said ... *Are? You? Sleeping*?"

She sat up and rubbed her eyes. "Now I'm not."

"Me, neither," I sighed.

"What's wrong?" she asked.

I shrugged. "Nothing."

She slid back down and snuggled back under the covers, shutting her eyes.

I sighed. "It's just ... well ... are you worried about what's going to happen after Saturday?" I blurted out. "After they get married?"

She opened her eyes. "You mean am I worried that The Change might happen?"

I sat up and turned on the light. "*You* know about the Change, too?"

"Everyone knows about blended families and The Change," she replied.

Um, everyone but *me*.

She sat up, too. "Lucy, this wedding—all it's doing is making it legal," she said. "Plus, The Change already did happen."

"It did?"

"Yeah, back in April when we moved in together."

"What do you mean?"

"Because that's when we all got to know each other," she explained. "And see each other when we were in bad moods. And fight. And make up. You know, like all families do." She yawned. "So the wedding part, it's really just an excuse to eat cake. That's all."

I looked over at her. There she was—the most popular girl in the world, with zit cream on her face and a mouth guard over her teeth to stop her from grinding them. "You know, for someone who spends most of her time pretending, you know a lot about this real-life stuff," I said.

She shrugged. "I learned it from you." She yawned again. "Now can I go back to sleep?"

"Okay," I replied. "Good night . . . *sis*."

It felt kind of cool rolling off my tongue like that. Like a whistle or something. It was so cool that I kept whispering it over and over. At least until Laurel told me that if I didn't be quiet she'd have to hurt me.

Which felt like a very sister-like thing to say.

chapter 10

Dear Dr. Maude,

Maybe you've already been to Vermont. But if you haven't, all I can say is that while Vermont may be really pretty, unless you like skiing, there's nothing to do. Especially when you're staying somewhere without cable or Internet. (Have you ever heard of this thing called dial-up? That's what Bill and Lois have. According to Alan, it's how people used to have to connect to the web in the old days, through a phone line. It's VERY slow.)

Because there's nothing to do, we were able to spend an entire day full of family quality time together yesterday. Well, family and TV crew quality time. (Ask Wendi to tell you about how she screamed at her assistant Charles during Charades.) (Actually, don't ask her, because she'd probably be embarrassed about that.)

Luckily, now it's Friday, which means everyone will be here for the wedding in a little while. I'm a little nervous about having Beatrice and Marissa in the same room together. As I've mentioned, Marissa is REALLY annoying. And while I can handle her because I'm just used to her by now, Beatrice, because she's a born-and-bred New York, isn't all that patient with people who are annoying on a Marissa-like level.

Hopefully, it'll be okay. It kind of has to be because it's not like they can be split up and go stay in another hotel, like, say, a Hilton Garden Inn with an indoor pool and room service.

This might be weird to say, but now that the wedding is no longer just family, I wish you could be here, too. I know we haven't met yet, but I still feel very close to you.

yours truly,
LUCY B. PARKER

On Friday morning, I was sitting in the living room with Lois, going through her scrapbook with pictures from last year's apple festival (she won second place for her apple cobbler), waiting for Pete's silver Oldsmobile to pull up with him and Rose and Beatrice. Which would explain why I got so confused when, instead, the car that pulled up was Beatrice's moms' black Mercedes station wagon. And I was even more confused when the car doors opened and not only did her two moms get out, along with Beatrice and Pete and Rose, but SO DID BLAIR LERNER-MOSKOWITZ.

"OH MY GOD!" I screamed when I saw him jump out of the back-back and wipe his face with his Pac Man T-shirt.

"I know, I know," Lois sighed. "I can't believe they gave the blue ribbon to Betty Miller, either. Don't get me wrong—I like Betty. But plain old apple pie should not be winning county fair contests." She sat up straight. "We have a reputation to uphold."

"No! That's not what I meant! What I meant was . . . I mean, I can't believe . . . I mean, what am I going to do . . . I mean . . . will you excuse me, please?" I babbled as I pulled my boots on the wrong feet and ran outside.

"Oh wow. Look who's here!" I said as I walked toward the car with a big fake smile on my face. I was so getting my period at that moment from the stress of this. I had to be. "It's Beatrice and Pete and Rose who were supposed to be here, and then the rest of the Lerner-Moskovitzes!" I turned to Rose. "Please tell me you have some fried plantains with you," I whispered.

She patted me on the cheek. "For my baby? Of course I do!" she said, whipping out a bag and handing it to me.

"Hey, Lucy," Blair said as he made his way to the door. "They have cable, right?"

How could he act so . . . *normal*?! "Actually, no. No, they don't," I replied. "But Bill's got a bunch of bowling shows taped if you want to watch those."

He shrugged. "Okay," he said as he walked in. I guess Mom was right when, once when I was overlistening to her talk to Deanna, I heard her say that men were very simple creatures.

"Beatrice, I had no idea all of the Lerner-Moskovitzes were coming," I said with the same fake smile on my face. "I thought it was just you."

She gave me a weird look. "Why are you talking like a flight attendant giving the safety speech?" she asked.

"I am not," I said, smiling.

Pete nodded. "*Chica*, she's right—you are."

I dropped the smile and looked over at Beatrice's moms, who had just finished checking the pressure on the tires (according to Pete, part of being a New Yorker included being neurotic) and were walking toward us. "Hello, Lucy," said her mom Marsha. "We're going to go inside and see if we can't get the owners of that bed-and-breakfast we booked the next town over on the phone."

"Okay," I said with my frozen smile.

After they were gone, I dropped it. "Beatrice, *what* is going on?" I cried. "What is your brother doing here?"

"I told you he was coming in the e-mail I sent you," she replied.

"What e-mail?"

"The one that said that my moms had decided that this would be a good way to have some quality family time—so everyone was going to come up."

"But there's no signal up here!" I said.

She shrugged. "That's probably why you didn't get it then."

How could she be so calm?! Pete patted me on the arm. "Don't worry, Lucy. There's no reason to be nervous, even though your local crush is gonna be staying in a bed-and-breakfast down the road for the weekend."

Marsha came to the door. "FYI, we have a little change of plans!" she said. "The other B and B mistakenly overbooked, but luckily there's an extra room here."

"Scratch that—your local crush is going to be staying under the same roof as you," Pete said.

Forget worrying about The Change, or what was going to happen when Beatrice and Marissa met. I now had even bigger things to worry about.

Team Northampton (Dad, Sarah, Ziggy, and Marissa) were the next to arrive. "OMIGOD OMIGOD OMIGOD!" Marissa screeched as she flew out of the car and ran straight toward Beatrice and threw her arms around her so hard she almost knocked her down. "I CAN'T BELIEVE I'M FINALLY MEETING YOU!"

Beatrice wiggled out of her embrace. "You must be Marissa," she said,

"Of COURSE I'm Marissa!" she cried. "Who else would I be?! This is SO cool! It's like meeting a BFF I never even knew I had! I just feel sooooo close to you already. It's like I've known you my entire life instead of just a minute."

Beatrice looked at me, panicked.

I shrugged. "I warned you," I whispered as I made my way to the car to pick up Ziggy. I felt a little bad leaving her there, but I needed to give my brother a kiss as soon as possible. When I got there, he was being all fussy and cry-y, but as soon as I picked him up, he quieted down.

Dad shook his head. "You really have that baby-whisperer vibe, Lucy," he said.

"You sure do," Sarah agreed. She squinted. "I think it's your aura. It's looking very purple."

According to Sarah and her weird friends, auras were your energy and they changed colors. Seeing that purple was my favorite color, that worked for me.

"Thanks," I said as Ziggy grabbed my index finger with his tiny fist.

"So how's it going?" Dad asked. "Your mom just told me that your local crush Blair Lerner-Moskovitz is here."

"What?!"

He nodded. "She called me about an hour ago and told me," he said. "So that we'd be prepared and not embarrass you about it."

Um, embarrass me? Kind of like he was doing at that moment? Did my divorced parents really have to communicate THAT much?

"How are you feeling about it?" he asked. "Is it making you uncomfortable? Because it really shouldn't. Crushes are a totally normal part of human development."

"It'll be fine," I said. "Well, it'll be fine as long as you stop talking about it."

He nodded. "Will do."

Just as we were about to go inside, a big Escalade pulled up. Laurel came flying out of house, almost tackling Austin as he got out of the truck. Jeez, if she wasn't careful she really *would* end up blind. As they ran into the house to catch up (forty-eight hours without being able to text had been super hard for her), Blair walked out.

"Hey, Lucy—you got any snacks lying around?" he asked. "All they have here is stuff made of apples. I hate apples. They're so . . . *healthy.*"

"Yeah. In my room. I'll go get them," I said as I followed him inside. Once I got up there, I crouched down so I was eye level with the doorknob. "Yeah, hi, Whoever's out there? It's me, Lucy B. Parker," I whispered. I had recently discovered that the whole praying business that people did really worked—even when you prayed to a doorknob instead of God or Buddha. Which was good because I wasn't sure how I felt about either of them. "I don't have a lot of time to talk, but I just wanted to know if You could help me get through the next few days with not too much embarrassment. Including the toast."

Before I could continue, I heard Ziggy start to cry. "And now I have to go, because my baby brother is crying and I'm the only one who can calm him down, but if I can, I'll be in touch later. Thanks a lot."

That night at dinner (apple and corn fritters, pork loin with braised apples, and apple rice pudding) Alan announced that all members of the Parker-Moses family would have IBS sessions the following morning before the wedding. ("Our last non-married ones.")

Marissa began to wave her hand wildly. "Oh! Oh! I have a question!"

Alan flinched. I don't think he had quite believed me when I told him how annoying Marissa was. "Yes, Marissa?"

"Can non-family members also have them?"

"Absolutely. In fact, I strongly encourage them," he replied.

She reached over and grabbed Beatrice's arm. "Good. I call Beatrice, then!"

From the look on her face, Beatrice would have rather spent her time picking splinters out of her finger.

Laurel's and Mom's would be spent with Laurel helping with hair and makeup while Alan and I would go see if we could find any flowers to make a bouquet for Mom. Although the fact that it was the beginning of November would make it kind of hard to do that. As far as I was concerned, I got the better end of the deal, because no matter how many times Laurel tried to say it was fun, putting on makeup was *really* boring. Even Camilla thought so, which is why the camera crew was going with us.

The next morning as we walked through the woods, Alan turned to me. "Lucy, there's something we need to talk about," he said as I began to make Mom a bouquet of pinecones.

I turned to him. "I don't know why you would automatically think *I* was the one who was eating chocolate-covered pretzels in the living room."

"What?" he asked confused.

"Nothing. You were saying?"

"Wait, wait," Wendi said. "Nikko, get the camera ready." Once he did, she looked into the lens. "People, at this moment—the day that Alan Moses and Rebecca Parker are to unite their two families—we're on a pre-wedding quality-time stroll with Alan and his soon-to-be stepdaughter, Lucy Parker—"

"Lucy *B.* Parker," everyone corrected.

"Lucy *B.* Parker," she repeated. "Okay, you can go back to bonding now."

He reached out and took my hand. "Lucy, you have no idea how lucky I feel that Laurel and I found you and your mom—"

"Are you getting this?!" Wendi asked Nikko.

"Yes, I'm getting it," he sighed.

Uh-oh. I could see Alan's eyes getting all watery. "I know. It's okay," I said, hoping to stop him from going on. For some reason it made me uncomfortable when grown men did what Mom called "getting in touch with their feelings." Especially when there was a video camera around. She said I'd appreciate it when I got older, but all it did now was make my neck itch.

"Laurel's never been happier in her life," he went on. "I tried the best I could to help her have a normal childhood, but it wasn't until you came around that she really learned how to have fun." He swiped at his eyes. "Lucy, you're very lucky that you have your dad. He's a wonderful person and I know I could never replace him, but I just hope . . . well, I hope that you know how much I love you." His eyes got all teary again. "I couldn't love you more if you were my own."

Now *I was* crying. "Thanks, Alan," I said, wiping at my own eyes. "I'm really glad Mom's marrying you. "'Cause even though she was always saying she was happy after she and Dad got divorced, I think she was lying sometimes. Because with you, she's *really* happy." I smiled. "And I am, too."

Due to the fact that she was so not into beauty stuff, Mom with makeup and nice hair didn't look all that different than Mom without makeup and nice hair. That being said, because she didn't want to run the risk of messing it up, for our IBS she didn't want to take a walk. Instead, she came up with what had to be the single most horrible idea I could think of .

"Me trying on bras is *not* my idea of a fun IBS!" I cried as she dumped out a Walmart bag full of them.

"Well, honey, if you stopped growing so quickly, we

wouldn't have to do this," she said, as if I had any control over the issue.

"When did you even get these?"

"When you and Laurel were posing with the Dairy Queen in front of the store," she said. "They were on sale."

The day before, after running out of things to do at the inn, we had taken a field trip to the local Walmart. (In Vermont, "local" meant forty-five minutes away.) It turned out that Laurel wasn't the only celebrity there—that year's Dairy Queen winner (dairy as in moo, cow, rather than ice cream) was, as well. Which, according to Martha from Walmart, meant the picture would be on the front page of the weekly paper for sure.

I sighed. I had enough experience to know that me trying to get myself out of this bra thing was not happening. At least it was just us. The first time I had gotten a bra it was at Barbara's Bra World in the Holyoke Mall, and Barbara had touched what she insisted on calling my boobies. The whole thing *still* gave me nightmares.

"Okay, off with it," Mom said, pointing to my sweater.

I shook my head as I grabbed a bunch of the bras. "I'll just take them into the bathroom."

"Oh," Mom said. "*Oh.*"

I stopped and turned. "Oh what?"

"Nothing," she said, her lip quivering.

Did all families cry this much or just mine?

"It's just . . ." A few tears dripped out of her eyes, kind of like our leaky kitchen faucet back in Northampton. "You're just . . ." Then, as if someone had turned on the one in our kitchen in New York—the one with the awesome water pressure—the tears came full force. ". . . getting so grown up!" she wailed. "And I'm not talking about your breasts!"

So much for her makeup. Even though there was no one else in the room, I still wanted to crawl under the bed and hide. I was glad that Wendi was off filming Laurel and Alan browsing through the most recent Container Store catalog, because I did *not* need all of America hearing about my breasts.

"I'm not *that* grown up," I said, in hopes of getting her to stop crying. "I haven't even gotten my period yet."

She reached for a tissue. "I'm talking about your attitude," she sniffled before she honked into it. "To watch how you've dealt with so much change this year, and how, even when you've been scared—like when you had to change schools, or when you were running for class president—you've just walked through it." She honked again. "Lucy, I don't think you know how brave you are."

"But I don't feel so brave sometimes," I admitted. "Sometimes I feel very . . . *not* brave. Like with this whole Change thing."

"What's The Change?" Mom asked.

It made me feel a little better than there was someone

on the planet who didn't know what it was. "Apparently it's this thing that happens when people get remarried," I explained. "And suddenly everything changes and no one's on their best behavior anymore and the kids who aren't loved as much as the other ones get sent away to boarding school."

"Is that what you think is going to happen to you?" Mom asked. "That we're going to send you away?"

"*No*," I said defensively. "Okay, fine, *yes*," I admitted. "Maybe sometimes I worry about that."

She came over and pulled me toward her. "Lucy, no one's going anywhere. We're a family, okay? Sometimes families fight, and sometimes they get annoyed with each other, but, like it or not, family is forever."

Just then my phone—which I had put in the corner near the door along with everyone else's, because we had figured out that that was the only place in the entire place where you got service—beeped with a text. I walked over and grabbed it. "It's from Alice," I said nervously. She was feeding Miss Piggy and Dr. Maude while we were gone. And making sure Miss Piggy didn't kill Dr. Maude. *Thought u'd want to see this*, it said underneath a photo. I clicked on it. "I can't believe it," I gasped. Instead of being a photo of something out of a horror movie, it looked like a page from one of those cute animal calendars. A sleeping Miss Piggy and Dr. Maude, curled together like some sort of giant fluff ball.

Mom looked at it and laughed. "Well, there you go.

Sometimes it takes a while for some of the members to come around, but they do. Eventually."

I don't know if there are a lot of wedding videos where the ceremony has to be stopped so one of the maids of honor (me) can take hold of a crying baby (Ziggy) because she's the only one with baby-whispering powers. But this one—with a title card that read "A film by Blair Lerner-Moskovitz"—had that. It also had a ponytailed wedding officiant (Dad) who used to be married to the bride (Mom) who cried through a long-bordering-on-too-long speech about the beauty of being able to watch your ex-wife find new love while his new baby mama (Sarah) cried along with him.

Laurel leaned over. "Is it just me or is all of this just a little weird?" she whispered.

"It's not a little weird," I whispered back. "It's *a lot* weird."

As Dad went on and on comparing life to flower petals before shushing Marissa, who wouldn't stop whispering to a glum-looking Beatrice, I looked longingly at the tray of turkey and apple roll-ups that Lois had prepared as little pre-wedding hors d'oeuvres, and wondered if it would be considered really rude if I walked over and took some. For the last hour I had had hunger pains—a whole new experience for me because I never actually let myself get hungry. I had always heard they were sharp, but these were more constant and made me feel like I was going to throw up. And not just because a few times when I had glanced over at Blair I had caught him looking at me first.

And then it happened.

I was trying to pay attention to Dad's story about Buddha, who lived a gazillion years ago, and how that tied in with modern-day families, but when the dripping feeling started, I got a little sidetracked. I felt the bottom of Ziggy's diaper, but it was dry. So what was going on? I had purposely avoided drinking anything for an hour before the ceremony so that I wouldn't have to go to the bathroom in the middle of it, but that didn't seem to matter. While my baby brother was able to hold his bladder, apparently I—his older sister—could not.

I tried to casually cross one leg in front of the other in an effort to stop the dripping, but *casually* was not something I had a lot of experience with, which explained why I bumped into Laurel.

Laurel gave me a look. "What are you doing?" she whispered.

"I have to go to the bathroom," I hissed.

"Can't you just wait until the ceremony's over?"

More dripping. Like a lot.

Um, no. I couldn't just sneak out; there were only a few people here. So I raised my hand. "Excuse me. I hate to do this, but I really have to go to the bathroom," I announced.

"But I was just about to read a poem by a seventeenth-century Sufi mystic," Dad said.

"You can e-mail it me," I yelled over my shoulder as I ran toward the bathroom.

I had thought I was done with Incidents-with-capital-*I*'s. First the Straightening Iron one, then the Hat one, and now the Peeing-in-My-Pants-During-My-Parents'-Wedding one. That one was so long I was going to have to abbreviate it to PIMPDMPW.

But as I looked at my underwear I realized I was wrong. This would not go down in history as the PIMPDMPW Incident.

Yes, this was my parents' wedding day. But just as importantly, it would go down in history as the day that the Period Incident occurred.

I looked at my watch. November 4, 2:17 p.m. Finally—FINALLY—I had something to enter in the "Official Period Log of the Girls at the Center for Creative Learning."

Armed with two Advil (they were period cramps—not hunger pains!) and a maxipad topped by a minipad, I made my way back to the ceremony.

"Is everything okay?" Alan asked anxiously.

"Yup," I said.

"You're sure?" Mom asked.

"Uh-huh," I said, trying to keep a straight face when what I really wanted to do, if I hadn't been tone deaf, was break into song. "So, uh, where are we?"

Laurel looked at me. "*Oh. My. God*," she gasped.

I couldn't believe she knew what had happened. Actually, I could. It was a frister thing. I broke into a huge grin. "Uh-huh."

"What?" Marissa demanded. "What is it? What's 'Oh my God'?" She turned to Beatrice. "Do you know what they're talking about? What did we miss?"

Beatrice's eyes were glazed over, as if she had left her body like twenty minutes earlier.

"Nothing," Laurel and I said at the same time.

"So where are we?" I asked.

"We're just about to do the vows," Dad said. He turned to Mom and me. "Rebecca and Lucy, do you two take Alan and Laurel to be your lawfully wedded husband, daughter, father, and sister?"

She turned to me. "What do you think, Lucy?"

I smiled. "Okay." I balled my hands into fists in an attempt to stop myself from adjusting my maxipad. You'd think with all the time I had spent practicing with them it wouldn't feel so weird but it did.

Dad turned to Alan and Laurel. "Alan and Laurel, what about you guys? Do you two take Rebecca and Lucy to be your lawfully wedded wife, daughter, mother, and sister?"

"We do," Laurel answered.

Maybe it was hormones, but I couldn't help myself—I started to cry. And I didn't care that I was being filmed not just by a TV crew but by my local crush.

"Well, then, there you have it—I now pronounce you a family. You can ... all hug!"

And we did. For a very long time.

For the rest of the day, whenever I did something, I couldn't help but think: *This is the first fill-in-the-blank I've had/done since I got my period.*

This is the first apple pig in a blanket I've had since I got my period.

This is the first time I've suffered through Marissa rambling since I got my period.

This is the first toast I've given at a wedding since I got my period. (Actually, it was the first toast I had given at a wedding ever.)

This is the first time I've danced with a boy who is not my frather since I got my period.

And, in that case, that was the first time I had danced with a boy, *period.*

"They sure eat a lot of apples up here, huh?" Blair asked after dinner as we picked at our apple pie à la mode (with apple ice cream, natch).

"Yeah. I guess." *That was the first time I said, "Yeah. I guess," after getting my period*, I thought to myself.

After flipping through Bill and Lois's limited CD collection, Alan pulled one out. "Ooh—I love this one!" he cried. "And I know just what song to put on." As he put it in the boom box, the sounds of some guy singing about not being able to smile without someone filled the living room.

"What is this?" I asked warily. The last time Alan had chosen the music, at the mock dance he had put together for me and him on the night of the Sadie Hawkins one, he had chosen Neil Diamond doing a sad duet with some lady named Barbra Streisand about how they didn't bring each other flowers anymore.

"It's Barry Manilow," he replied. "'Can't Smile Without You.'"

Blair looked at me. "Never heard of the guy."

"Me, neither," I replied.

As we sat there, Mom and Alan began to dance, followed by Laurel and Austin and then Dad and Sarah and then Pete and Rose. Even Bill and Lois got into it. Beatrice and Marissa were off in the other room watching *Antique Roadshow* on PBS. ("Anything to drown out her talking," Beatrice had said.)

"So, uh, you want to?" Blair asked, staring at the ground.

"Do I want to what?" I replied.

He gave a long sigh. "Dance!" he said, all upset.

"Jeez. You don't have to get all huffy," I said, just as upset.

"Well, do you?"

I shrugged. "I guess."

We stood up and made our way to the dance floor, which was really just a sliver of space near the coffee table.

"So how do we do this?" Blair asked.

I looked around at everyone else. "I think you take your hands and put them on my hips, and I take mine and put them on your shoulders."

He looked doubtful. "Are you sure?"

"I don't know! It's not like I've ever done this before. I mean, with someone who wasn't an almost-parent."

He reached out and put his hands near my hips without exactly touching them. They just kind of . . . *hovered* there.

"Are we going to do this or not?" I asked. "Because we don't have to, you know. We could just—"

"Okay, okay," he said, grabbing them so tight I'm surprised he didn't squeeze the maxipad off of me.

"Ow."

Once he loosened up on them, I reached up and put my hands on his shoulders. Or, rather, *near* his shoulders.

"I shouldn't be the only one who's doing this, you know," he said.

"Fine," I said, holding on to them as little as possible. Once we had bodily contact on both ends, we both relaxed a bit and began to . . . well, it wasn't exactly dancing. It was more like we moved from side to side, sometimes in rhythm, but mostly not. With a lot of stepping on each other's toes.

"Don't take this the wrong way, but is this supposed to be fun?" he asked.

I shrugged. "I think so. But you want to stop and go through my snack supply?"

"Yes," he said as he quickly let go of me and headed for the stairs.

Okay, so maybe I couldn't say I had danced with a boy for the first time. But still, it was something. At least I was on my way. And at least I had had my period when it happened.

As I got to the stairs I stopped and turned around.

There they were—my family. Some who had given birth to me; some I lived with now; and some who weren't actually related to me but whom I still loved as if they were. To other people, it may have sounded confusing when I tried to explain how we all fit together, but to me?

It made perfect sense.

chapter 11

Dear Dr. Maude,

I don't know if you remember me. I'm the girl who lives upstairs and used to write you e-mails. You know—the ones that you never replied to? I know—it's been, like, six months since I've written to you. (Can you believe it's already April and I've been living in New York City for a year?! I can't.) Sorry about that. It's just that (a) after the wedding my life got really, REALLY busy, and (b) I guess now that I'm so much wiser—you know, seeing that I now GET MY PERIOD AND ALL—I realized that the chances of you writing back to me are about as great as me waking up with my hair down to my butt. (Not that that won't happen at some point, but it'll probably take at least four years.)

Anyway, if for whatever reason you do read these e-mails and just don't respond to them because, I don't know, you just don't, but the fact that they're no longer appearing in your in-box makes you sad, then I'm sorry. But like I said, things have just been crazy.

First of all, other than everyone eating a lot of apples over the weekend, the wedding went very smoothly. When Blair Lerner-Moskovitz showed up, I didn't think it would, but it did. We even kind-of, sort-of danced together for a second. Since then we've been hanging out. Not really in a boyfriend/girlfriend way (I'm not even exactly sure what that would mean, but I just intuitively know—probably because I AM NOW A GIRL WHO GETS HER PERIOD and therefore has excellent intuition—that that's not what it is. Maybe because there's no kissing involved.)

Instead we do things like go for walks in Central Park and to different bakeries around town. And next weekend we're going to ComicCon (have you heard of it? It's a comic book festival) which, to be honest, I do NOT want to go, but I am because sometimes with friends you do things they want to do. Even if you have no interest. Laurel says that we're just taking it slow, which is a good thing and the best basis for a relationship. At least that's what all the articles in the magazines she reads say. I'm not in a hurry or anything. I'm just happy I have his name in the crush log. Although I still have to find boys for the other two crushes . . .

I got back from the wedding to a ton of e-mails from kids needing advice. Because my fingers got all crampy typing up the responses, I came up with an idea that I hope doesn't make you feel like I'm a total copycat when you hear it. In order not to have to type so much, I decided that once a week, I would hold a meeting after school where kids could come and ask their questions and get advice right then and there. It's not filmed and aired on TV, so it's not like I'm COMPLETELY copying you and I have my own show or anything, but I guess it's a little like what you do.

Well, it totally took off. To the point where I had to move it from the classroom where Spanish class is held to the cafeteria. I don't think you've ever been to my school, but if you had, you would know that the cafeteria is REALLY big. It doesn't get completely filled, but sometimes it's close. I'm even thinking of continuing it during summer break.

So, as you can imagine from your own show (not that this is an actual show), I'm very busy. Plus, ever since the *Week with Wendi* episode aired back in February, I've been getting a lot of e-mails from different kids around the country asking me for advice about their own blended-family issues. I don't know if you're aware of this, but there are a lot of us blended-family kids. In fact, not to tell you what to do, but you might want to do an episode on that subject.

I don't know if you saw it, but the show turned out great. There was some stuff with Mom acting all stressy, but it was balanced with footage where we were all getting along and acting goofy. I guess to the average viewer, we may seem a little weird, but according to Mom, EVERY family is weird in its own way. For someone who isn't big on reality shows (unless she's super stressed out about getting married), Mom was very happy with how it turned out.

Marci—that's Laurel's publicist—got the network to agree to repeat the episode again in January right before the Academy votes for the Oscars. Hopefully it'll help. Although from the dailies of the movie that Laurel let me see, she won't need any help at all because her performance is AWESOME.

(In case you don't know what dailies are, that's the footage from the day's shooting on a movie or TV show.)

Well, I should get going. Beatrice is coming over so we can take photos of Miss Piggy and Dr. Maude to submit to this Animal BFFs contest I saw advertised on the Animal Planet website. They're so BFF now it's a little on the nauseating side. I know I said I wanted a kitten to make up for the fact that my other cat hated me, but I didn't think about the fact that THIS would happen.

I hope everything's good for you. This is going to sound weird, but even though you never wrote me back, you've really helped me over the last few years. It's hard to explain, but just knowing you're out there somewhere has made me feel better as I've dealt with stuff.

Maybe we'll run into each other in the elevator one day. Or not.

yours truly,
Lucy B. Parker

When I'm not busy overlistening to my mom's conversations or keeping the Official Crush Log of the Center for Creative Learning, I'm updating my website!

LUCYBPARKER. COM

Check out my site for:

- A sneak peek at upcoming books

- My personal "Why Me?" diary

- The purr-fectly funny "As Seen by Miss Piggy" feature

- Author Robin Palmer's advice column (She's a LOT better at responding than Dr. Maude!)

- Fun downloadables and more exclusive content!

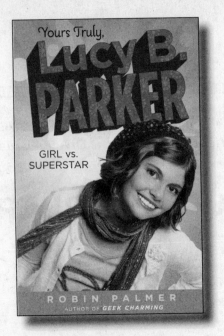

Yours Truly,
LUCY B. PARKER

GIRL vs. SUPERSTAR

ROBIN PALMER
AUTHOR OF *GEEK CHARMING*

1: Girl vs. Superstar

Sixth grade is hard enough for Lucy B. Parker, but it gets so much worse when her mom announces that she's going to marry Laurel Moses's dad. Yes, *that* Laurel Moses—the TV-movie-music star. All Lucy wants is to just get through the day without totally embarrassing herself, but that's hard to do when you're the less-pretty, less-talented not-quite-sister of a mega superstar.

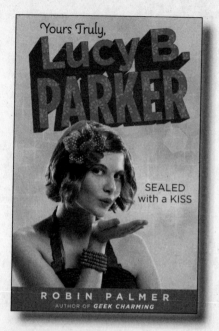

Yours Truly,

Lucy B. PARKER

SEALED
with a KISS

ROBIN PALMER

AUTHOR OF *GEEK CHARMING*

2: Sealed with a Kiss

Lucy B. Parker is spending her summer vacation off in L.A., visiting Laurel on the set of her new movie and meeting teen heartthrobs left and right. Life is good, until Lucy develops a crush—and unlike previous crushes, this one is not on a character in a book or a movie, but on a real living, breathing boy. Unfortunately for Lucy, nothing ever seems to go as she plans.

3: Vote for Me!

Lucy B. Parker is running for class president! And she's up against the most popular girl in school. Sure, Lucy could let her frister (friend + sister), teen superstar Laurel Moses, campaign for her, but Lucy wants to win as *Lucy*. How is Lucy going to manage the campaign of the year?

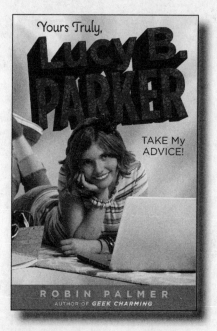

4: Take My Advice!

When Lucy becomes the advice columnist for her school paper, she suddenly has a lot more on her plate than she bargained for. Lucy's not really sure how she's going to pull this off, but with the Sadie Hawkins dance coming up, it seems like everyone in her class needs some help.

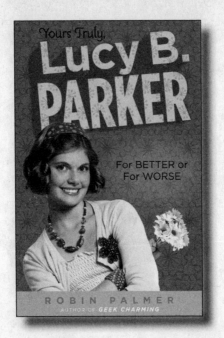

5: For Better or For Worse

When Lucy's mom and soon-to-be stepdad announce that they're finally getting married—in a month—Lucy's life turns upside down. Wedding planning is hard enough, but when a reality TV crew ends up following the family around while it's happening, the results are disastrous. Can Lucy save the day—not to mention, the family—or will everything fall apart?

Get Hooked
ON THESE OTHER
FABULOUS
Girl Series!

Lucy B. Parker: Girl vs. Superstar
By Robin Palmer

Forever Four
By Elizabeth Cody Kimmel

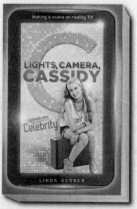

Lights, Camera, Cassidy: Episode 1: Celebrity
By Linda Gerber

Almost Identical
By Lin Oliver

Check out sample chapters at
http://tinyurl.com/penguingirlsampler

Grosset & Dunlap • Puffin Books • Divisions of Penguin Young Readers Group
www.penguin.com/youngreaders